GUS AND GLORY

Also by Sarah Guillory
Nowhere Better Than Here

GUS AND GLORY

SARAH GUILLORY

ROARING BROOK PRESS
New York

Published by Roaring Brook Press
Roaring Brook Press is a division of
Holtzbrinck Publishing Holdings Limited Partnership
120 Broadway, New York, NY 10271 • mackids.com

Text copyright © 2025 by Sarah Guillory.
Chapter opener spots © Shutterstock. All rights reserved.

Our books may be purchased in bulk for promotional, educational, or business use. Please contact your local bookseller or the Macmillan Corporate and Premium Sales Department at (800) 221-7945 ext. 5442 or by email at MacmillanSpecialMarkets@macmillan.com.

Library of Congress Control Number: 2024026022

First edition, 2025
Book design by L. Whitt
Printed in the United States of America by Lakeside Book Company,
Harrisonburg, Virginia

ISBN 978-1-250-34936-1
1 3 5 7 9 10 8 6 4 2

In memory of Rosemary Harris,
a teacher who gave so much of
herself to provide me with opportunities
I wouldn't have had otherwise.
Thank you for sharing your time,
talents, and wisdom.

And in memory of my own dog Gus,
who made my life so much better and
my house so much dirtier.
I miss you, boy.
Yes, even the slobber.

CHAPTER ONE

The summer I was twelve, my mom got lost. My dad told me she was just on vacation, but I wouldn't have bought that story even if it had only cost a nickel. I, like all great detectives, was a seeker of truth, and this didn't feel like the whole truth at all. It felt like a thin version of the truth, a layer of sugar dusted over oatmeal to make the whole thing easier to swallow.

Not that my dad was a liar—he wasn't. But he was an adult, and if I had learned anything in my twelve years, it was that adults could be stingy with the truth. They'd drop a bite here or a crumb there, but they never gave out the whole thing, just in case we might get hungry for more.

That was because most adults underestimated kids. Maybe it wasn't entirely their fault. It was just that they could be very shortsighted sometimes, bless their hearts.

I, on the other hand, was not at all shortsighted. It was how I knew my mom wasn't really on vacation.

I took the last pair of shorts from my suitcase and tucked them into an old dresser. My dad had dropped me off at my grandparents' house three days ago, but I hadn't wanted to unpack, despite Nana Pat offering to help. A part of me kept expecting Mom to pull up, ready to go, so I'd kept everything packed just in case.

But she'd been gone for three weeks, and I couldn't live out of a suitcase forever.

I unearthed the stack of postcards my dad had sent me from the road. He was a long-haul truck driver and always picked ones he thought I'd get a kick out of. He once sent me one from a place in Arkansas called Booger Holler. Another from Toad Suck, Arkansas. (Apparently there wasn't much normal about Arkansas.) Sweet Lips, Tennessee. The postcards had funny pictures or strange roadside attractions or celebrated the most uninteresting buildings.

These postcards had always made Mom mad. She would grumble about having to work two jobs to pay the rent while Dad went gallivanting off. At least I didn't have to hide the postcards under my bed anymore. I tacked them up on the empty bulletin board hanging on the wall.

With Mom gone and Dad on the road, I was spending the summer with my mom's parents in Sweet Olive, Louisiana. The room itself was so far the best part about having to be here. It was much bigger than my room at home. The walls at my grandparents' were painted white, and the ceiling was sloped and came to a point right above my head. Small circular windows faced each other on either side of the long, narrow room. I had a white iron bed topped with a colorful quilt.

My bedroom in my and Mom's apartment in Baton Rouge had thin walls, which meant I could hear the neighbors

screaming at each other in the middle of the night. The ceiling had a mildew stain where the roof leaked. Our landlord kept saying he was going to fix it, but he never did.

Mom said you couldn't trust a word a landlord said. That was why she didn't ever feel bad about being late with the rent. But sometimes she got so late that we had to find another place to stay. I'd lived in at least five different apartments in my twelve years.

But Nana Pat and Papaw Jack had lived in this house for thirty-five.

My grandparents weren't telling me where Mom was either. I suspected everyone in my life of hiding the full truth of what was going on. I'd read enough detective novels to know that much. But I doubted Nana Pat and Papaw Jack knew much of anything. Mom and I hadn't seen them in over a year.

My room at the top of the stairs was quiet, and I'd learned over the past three days that this might have been the quietest house I'd ever been in. I worried my voice might fade from lack of use.

I picked up my phone and tried to call Mom again. The robot voice told me her number was no longer in service. It had been saying that since the day she'd left. I called Dad but got his voicemail. I tossed my phone on the bed. I'd run out of people to call.

I unpacked my books. Most of them were old, edges worn and frayed, pages discolored. They came from thrift stores or library sales, loved by somebody else before they were loved by me.

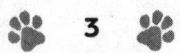

Sometimes I practiced my detective skills with books, attempting to see if I could guess, based on what they'd left behind, something about who that person was—had they liked dogs, eaten peanut butter and banana sandwiches, lived near the beach or the mountains or in a big city? But all I'd managed to figure out from this book was that whoever had owned it first had dog-eared the pages.

I set my books on the mostly empty bookshelf in the corner of the room. I picked up one of the other books already on the shelf and opened it. My mom had scribbled her name across the inside cover.

A little current of electricity skittered across my skin. Funny how the familiar could do that. It was as if I'd just spotted my mom's face in a crowd.

I ran my finger over her name. Why hadn't she taken her books with her when she'd moved out?

I had a lot of whys to ask Mom. My unanswered questions lined up like cars in a traffic jam. Right now, they weren't going anywhere.

But I was good at puzzles, and I liked how the tiny pieces didn't look like much but when put all together showed a bigger picture. Mystery books were like that too. They gave you really small clues that seemed like nothing until, all of a sudden, they showed something.

Maybe I could put together all the tiny pieces of what I knew about Mom and see the bigger picture of why she left.

And if she was ever coming back.

I put the book back on the shelf. I needed out of this room. I flipped off the light and headed downstairs.

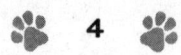

I tiptoed past the den; I didn't want to bother Papaw Jack. The den was dim, but I could see him sitting in his recliner. The TV was on, but it didn't look like he was really watching it.

Papaw Jack had had a stroke a little over a year ago, and he was mostly okay, just had some trouble with his right side. Sometimes it took a while for him to find the word he wanted to say. He spoke really slow and sometimes his words blurred together. Nana Pat said that was called dysarthria, and she would know. It wasn't that he couldn't speak or that he didn't—but when words were really hard, you had to decide if they were worth saying. I bet Papaw Jack hardly ever said anything he regretted, since he had to think it over and decide if it was worth it. He would make a good detective. He probably wouldn't ever give himself away, and he spent way more time listening than talking.

Not that he'd been much of a talker before his stroke. Even though I hadn't seen them in over a year, and not all that much even before that, the one thing I remembered about Papaw Jack was his laugh. His face would crack open, his eyes alight, and he would laugh long and loud.

I hadn't heard that reckless laughter in a while.

Nana Pat was bustling around the kitchen. She was always bustling or hustling, unable to sit still long. "I'm off to the hospital," she said by way of hello. She wore scrubs, and her salt-and-pepper hair was pulled into a ponytail. She was a nurse, and she'd gone part-time only after Papaw Jack's stroke. If you lined fifty people up in a row and asked a random stranger to point to whoever was in charge, I was pretty sure they would say it was Nana Pat. She just looked like she knew the best way to tile a bathroom and roast a chicken and get more funding for her department. It was a little intimidating. "Need something before I go?" She glanced at her watch and grimaced. "I can fix you some lunch real quick."

I didn't want to be any extra work for anyone. Besides, I'd spent a lot of time by myself at home. "I can do it."

"You're going to be okay?" she asked. That question had a whole lot of branches to it. I ignored most of them and just nodded. I would be okay.

Nana Pat had taken off work the first two days I was here to help me get settled, but I'd spent a lot of time in my room not unpacking and she'd spent a lot of time buzzing around the house and working in the garden.

"You call me if you need anything. Papaw Jack will want a nap after lunch, so don't be too loud or make him nervous." She glanced at her watch again. "I'll bring home something for dinner."

"I'll be fine," I told her. Told myself.

And then she was gone, and I had the long, hot day stretching out in front of me.

I didn't want to disturb Papaw Jack's nap, so I decided to fix myself a sandwich and walk down to the park on the corner. I remembered that place from before. My mom used to push me on the swings until her arms got tired. This was right after my parents divorced, so I was really little, and though it was a hazy memory, it was a good one.

I got the bread and peanut butter out of the pantry and found strawberry jelly in the fridge. It felt weird digging around in someone else's kitchen, even if that kitchen was vaguely familiar. The same blue curtains hung over the sink. A bulletin board hung on the wall near an old phone, and pinned up on the board were reminders for doctor appointments and invitations to weddings and old pictures. They had one of me from two years ago, but they also had one of me and my mom when I was a baby. It was starting to roll up at the edges.

I wrapped my sandwich in a paper towel and grabbed a cold drink from the fridge. I started down the hallway to tell Papaw Jack I was going to the park, but his snores drifted out of the den.

I left without telling him. He wouldn't know I was gone anyway.

Nana Pat and Papaw Jack's neighborhood was tidy but older. Tall trees lined the cracked sidewalk. A house two down from Nana Pat's needed painting, but their flower beds were pretty and colorful. A man in a very large hat was putting birdseed in a feeder. I smiled and waved, but he must not have seen me, because he didn't wave back.

Going unnoticed was good for detectives. They could see and hear so much more that way.

The park on the corner was very different from the one I remembered. The playground equipment was gone. The grass was shaggy and trash gathered in small piles at the edges. It was lonely and neglected. The new park on the other side of town must have attracted all the people. I sat on a weathered bench and stared at the broken concrete that showed where the swings had been.

It felt like I was the only person left on the planet.

My stomach grumbled. I unwrapped my sandwich and took a bite.

And that was when I heard something big crashing through the bushes.

CHAPTER TWO

My heart sped up a little as I squinted into the bushes. Clue number one: Whatever it was, it had fur. The leaves on the bush quivered and shook.

There was no need for me to collect clue number two. A branch snapped, and the mystery was solved.

Out stepped the wrinkliest dog I'd ever seen.

His face looked a little like melted ice cream. The folds of his skin puddled on his forehead and covered his eyes. He was a beautiful reddish-brown color, and his skin rolled like the ocean when he walked. He kept his head down, sniffing, and I thought he might actually step on those long, floppy ears of his. He was a big dog, and I was pretty sure he was too well fed to be a stray. Sure enough, when he got closer, I could see a collar.

He lifted his head and sniffed the air. His head swung in my direction. I was fairly certain he'd smelled my sandwich before he'd seen me.

He was alone, just like me. He lumbered across the park, taking the time to smell a hamburger wrapper, a plastic cup, and two clumps of grass. Nothing about this dog said fast. He sniffed at the air again, this time close enough that I could hear his nose just a-working.

His wrinkled, mushy face was both dignified and sad, and all I wanted to do was drop down in front of him and scratch those long hound ears. But I wasn't stupid. He was a strange dog, so I let him come to me.

And since I was holding a peanut butter and jelly sandwich, he wasn't shy at all. He walked right up to me and licked his lips.

"Hello. Are you lost?" Until now, I hadn't spoken to anyone but Nana Pat and Papaw Jack since Dad dropped me off.

The dog's tail wagged madly. He walked closer and dropped to a sit right in front of me.

"Well, aren't you handsome?" I gave him the top of my hand to sniff. The older lady who lived in the trailer next to Dad's had taught me what to do when meeting a strange dog for the first time. She had several big dogs and I used to go and play with them on the weekends I visited Dad. Sometimes she'd even let me take them for a walk around the trailer park.

This dog was now close enough that I could see the name *Gus* stamped on his collar, along with an address. So, he definitely wasn't a stray. He wagged his tail again, and taking that as permission, I gently rubbed his ear. He closed his eyes and leaned into my hand.

"What a polite way to ask for a pet," I told him. "You have very good manners."

He leaned toward my sandwich. I moved it out of the way just as his mouth snapped shut.

"Okay, maybe you have only so-so manners and a whole lot of confidence."

He huffed. Then he reached up and put his paw on my knee.

I laughed. "Gus, are you trying to sweet-talk me into my sandwich?"

He didn't look ashamed at his blatant use of puppy-dog eyes.

"I'm not so sure you can have a sandwich," I told him. "I don't think peanut butter and jelly is good for dogs."

He patted me with his paw again and tilted his head, telling me that yes, sandwiches were absolutely good for dogs, he would be happy to show me.

"Fine," I said. I looked to see if his owner would make an appearance. Nobody else was around. "But you better not tell anyone."

He licked his lips.

I tore off a piece of my sandwich. I had a moment of doubt as I held it out to him, afraid he might take my fingers with it, but he was surprisingly gentle as he plucked the bite from my palm.

He smacked his lips as the sandwich stuck to the roof of his mouth. I laughed, my voice loud in the otherwise quiet neighborhood. A nearby bird flew away, but nobody else noticed.

"Where did you come from?" And where was his person? He shouldn't have been wandering across streets alone.

He cocked his head, and I nibbled my sandwich. He

followed my hand with his eyes. I sighed and gave him my last bite.

This time he didn't bother chewing.

"You should have made it last longer," I told him. "That's all you're getting."

Now that I was out of food, Gus wandered off, checking out the trash can and a group of trees right behind me.

"You're going to get yourself in trouble." I got to my feet and carefully picked up some of the trash that had fallen on the ground. I balanced it on top of the other trash in the overfull can.

Gus had been sniffing the same spot for a while, so I went to investigate. He was nosing a dollar bill. "Look what you found!" I picked it up and held it out to him. Realizing it wasn't food, he turned away.

I put the money in my pocket and sat in the grass near Gus. He flopped down beside me, panting. It was still early June, but it was already hot and humid, and being outside had to be accomplished in small doses, mostly taken before the sun came up and after it went down. I wished I had some water to share with Gus. He looked like he needed it.

My scalp prickled with the heat and maybe with a little anger. This beautiful, sweet dog deserved to be better taken care of. He shouldn't have been left alone.

If I had a dog like this, I'd take such good care of him. Then neither one of us would have to be alone.

A slight breeze cooled my face, and Gus rolled over on his side. I ran my hand along his ribs, and his eyes drifted shut.

The quiet was peaceful now, not lonely. But then Gus

lifted his head, listening to something I couldn't hear, and lumbered to his feet. He shoved his face into mine, maybe to make sure I wasn't hiding any more sandwiches. Then he turned and trotted out of the park.

"It was nice meeting you!" I called as I watched him go. I tried not to be sad as his tail disappeared around the corner.

It rained for the next three days. I worried about Gus, hoping he was somewhere dry. I read *Murder on the Orient Express* and was completely surprised by the ending. I watched one episode of *Wheel of Fortune* with Papaw Jack and called Mom's phone twelve times. The robot voice answered every single time.

Today when I picked up the phone, I called Dad. He answered this time.

"Glory Bee!"

"Hey, Dad. Where are you?"

"Outside Denver. You should see these mountains—some of them still have snow on them."

"In June?" We rarely even got snow in January.

"In June. And while I'll take the weather here any day, I sure do miss the food."

"Nana Pat made chicken stew last night." We ate at the table too. Mom and I had usually eaten in front of the TV. If we'd eaten together at all.

"Don't rub it in," he said. "I had a greasy burger from a truck stop last night."

Trucker food was not good. "You have to eat two vegetables tomorrow," I told him.

"That won't be easy."

"Ketchup doesn't count. And try to find a fruit."

"Peach cobbler?"

"You are hopeless." On the weekends when I stayed with Dad, we mostly ate out. His fridge never had vegetables. The kitchen in his trailer was small. If he did cook, it was a burger on the grill.

He laughed. "You settling in okay?"

At least I wasn't living out of a suitcase. "I'm okay. Have you heard anything—"

"I sent you a postcard yesterday," he said before I could get my question out. He stepped around the situation with Mom as if it were a snake about to strike. "But I won't tell you from where. It'll be a surprise."

"Can't wait."

Dad belonged on the road. Mom had apparently decided she belonged anywhere but here. And me? I was trying to fit into a space that hadn't been made for me. Nana Pat and Papaw Jack were trying, but they hadn't had a kid in their house for a long time. I still didn't know why that was, which made me a pretty poor detective.

I swallowed my sigh. Too many questions and not enough answers.

"Well, I guess I'll check in with you in a few days," Dad said.

"Okay. Drive safe!" I hung up the phone and leaned against the foot of the bed. The constant patter of rain over my head had stopped, and I hoped that meant it had finally cleared off. I wanted to walk down to the park. I couldn't see out the round windows in my room since they were up near the ceiling, so I put my shoes on, ever hopeful, and headed downstairs.

Papaw Jack was puttering around the kitchen. He wore khaki pants, a white T-shirt, and a quiet sort of competence. He had always been a big man, tall and broad shouldered, but now he was smaller somehow, like time had just whittled pieces of him away. His hands were large, all gnarled up and scarred from years of work.

"All right?" he asked me. It came out a little rough, but I understood him just fine.

"I'm good." I wondered how long you had to repeat something before it became true.

Papaw Jack was very careful as he poured himself a cup of coffee with his left hand. He didn't put anything in it, just took the mug over to the kitchen table and sighed as he sat down.

I glanced out the window. It had indeed stopped raining. A wooden fence ran around the tidy backyard. A neighbor, an old lady who was wearing a bright scarf over her head and tied under her chin, peered over the fence. I couldn't tell what she was looking at. Nana Pat had flowers everywhere, and a small vegetable garden grew in the back corner near a weathered shed.

Papaw Jack used to spend a lot of time out in that shed. Mom told me once that her dad could fix anything, from broken chairs to lawn mowers. But now the narrow path that led from the back porch to the shed had grown over with grass.

And we hadn't even visited last Christmas.

I did not know why Mom stopped visiting her parents. I did not know what made her walk away from our home—from me.

But I was going to find out.

"Have you heard from my mom?" I asked.

Papaw Jack stared into his coffee, like maybe he was looking for her in there. It took him a little longer to get his words out. When Papaw Jack talked, you had to be patient and know that the words were important. He paused longer than normal between words, and sometimes his head scrunched in frustration and I knew he was trying to remember what something was called. He didn't look at me when he finally spoke. "Not for a long time."

I waited, giving him the time and space to find more words. He got up from the table and carried his coffee to the sink. He poured what was left of it down the drain and rinsed his mug.

I didn't know Papaw Jack well enough to know if he was sad or mad or had given up on my mom completely. What I was certain of in that moment was that he wasn't going to say anything else.

"Can I walk down to the park?" I asked.

He nodded.

"Do you want to go?" I added. He hadn't left the house in three days either.

He shook his head. "Too slow."

"I can walk slow."

He shook his head again. "I'm going to rest."

I'd learned that for Papaw Jack, *rest* meant *nap*. He just didn't like calling it that.

"Okay. I won't stay too long."

He was already disappearing down the hall. "Be careful."

I shoved two cookies in my pocket before slipping out the front door. The heat after all that rain made it feel like I was standing in a steamed-up shower. It was gross, but I didn't want to stay inside any longer.

I'd just stepped inside the park, which looked even worse soggy than it did dry, when a car honked behind me, followed by the loud squeal of brakes. I spun around to see Gus trotting across the road. The car waited until he was on the sidewalk before driving away, but that had been close.

"I've been worried about you!" I told him. And obviously for good reason. "You have to be careful!"

Gus had his head down, sniffing the grass that edged the sidewalk, his long ears and numerous forehead wrinkles covering his eyes. No wonder he'd walked out in front of that car. When he was smelling, he could barely see where he was going. His leash trailed behind him, covered in mud. As a matter of fact, Gus was mostly covered in mud too.

It didn't take much detective work to figure out what had happened—he'd gotten away from his owner during his walk. And into every puddle along the way.

"Gus!" I said.

He jerked his head up. His ears swung back and forth, but he didn't come to me.

I hurried over and tried to grab his leash, but Gus bucked and bolted, skittering out of the way, his tongue lolling out of the side of his mouth in an unmistakable grin.

"Not funny. This isn't a game," I told him.

He jumped and pranced just out of reach, making quite clear that to him, this was indeed the best game.

I shrugged. "Fine." I took a cookie out of my pocket and waved it around a bit, hoping some of the smell would make its way to him. I took a very loud bite.

Gus was sitting in front of me within ten seconds. I stomped on his leash, then handed him the cookie. "You are such a sucker." I bent down and got a good grip on the leash.

He didn't really seem to care that he'd just gotten caught. He smacked his lips, as if telling me that the cookie was a fair trade for his freedom.

I examined his collar. Along with his name, his address was printed on the metal plate. Giselle Street was only one street over. I knew that because I'd been in charge of navigation when Dad had dropped me off, and it was the street we had to turn on before turning onto the one where Nana Pat and Papaw Jack lived.

"I wish you could stay awhile," I said. I'd been thinking about Gus for the last three days. "But I bet your people are worried about you." I knew I would've been.

He nosed my hand and I broke the other cookie in half and gave it to him. I put the rest of it in my pocket just in case.

"Now don't pull me down," I told Gus, whose shoulder came up to my waist. He was a very big dog.

Gus mostly kept his head down as we walked, and I could hear his nose working as he sniffed his way along the sidewalk. He didn't take any detours, though, and he seemed to know the way home. I had to walk extra fast to keep up.

For the first time since arriving in Sweet Olive, people saw me. They slowed down on the street to watch Gus and me walk by.

"Are you walking that dog or is he walking you?" a woman called out as I passed by her house.

"Both, I think!" I shouted back.

We were probably funny looking—I wasn't very tall to begin with, and Gus was practically the size of a pony.

We turned onto Giselle Street, and I started looking at numbers. "512," I muttered as we passed an older house that had vines growing up one side. We were looking for 208.

Gus walked faster as we got closer to his house, even though I wanted to slow down and stretch out my time with him. The walk back was going to feel much longer without him.

"208," I said aloud, reading it off the mailbox. The house was light blue with navy shutters that needed painting. The yard was small but neat. Gus tried to veer around the house, but I held tight to his leash and led him up the sidewalk and onto the front porch. Gus wagged his tail as I rang the doorbell.

I realized I was frowning. I tried to rearrange my face, but I was angry that Gus's owner wasn't keeping a better eye on him. Gus had almost gotten really hurt today.

When nobody answered, I knocked on the door. Gus paced eagerly.

"Maybe they're out looking for you," I said. Gus tried to pull me off the porch. "I think we should wait right here until your person gets back."

He looked up at me. I didn't budge. He paced. He whimpered.

"You're okay." I ran my hand along his back to reassure him.

Gus tugged harder at the leash, and this time I let him pull me off the porch and into the yard. He veered around the house. A weathered picket fence went around a tiny backyard. The gate was open. "Is that how you got out?" I asked. "Hello!"

"I'm here," a voice said, a little weakly, and I hurried into the backyard.

When I rounded the house, I found an old man lying at the bottom of a short set of busted steps.

And Gus had brought me to him.

CHAPTER THREE

"Are you okay?" I asked as I ran to the man. My mouth tasted metallic. All my anger drained right out of me, leaving more than enough room for shame. Gus's person was old and hurt, not neglectful.

Gus followed. He nuzzled the man and licked his face. The man moaned a little and pushed Gus gently away. "Yes, yes, you're a good boy, but don't break my other leg."

"Can I help you up?" I realized then that I probably couldn't get the man inside.

"My leg's busted, I think, and my pride. It's my fault. Gus here has been cooped up inside for days. He needed a walk. And then this dang step finally quit on me." He winced and his lips went white. He was breathing hard. "Thing's rotten. Should have changed it out a long time ago."

I wasn't so sure he needed to be talking. He looked awful. "My grandma's a nurse. Should I call her?"

"No. Better just call an ambulance," the man said. He looked thoroughly aggravated by it. "I couldn't get to the phone."

Luckily, my phone was in my back pocket. I dialed 911.

"911, what's your emergency?"

"I'm at 208 Giselle Street. The man here fell down the stairs and broke his leg. He can't get up."

"Okay. Stay calm."

Easy for her to say. But I was breathing a little fast, so I took a big, deep breath.

"What's your name?" the 911 operator asked.

"Glory St. Romain."

"Okay, Glory, the ambulance is on its way. Just stay on the line."

She asked more questions, like Was he breathing (that one scared me, but he was) and Did he bump his head? I couldn't answer that last one, so I handed the man the phone and filled a bowl I found on the side of the house with water for Gus.

"You were trying to tell me," I told Gus. "I'm sorry I wasn't listening."

Gus heard the sirens first, because he threw back his head and howled. He sounded a little like a siren himself.

The old man hung up the phone and handed it back to me.

"Thank you, Glory St. Romain," he said. "I'm Homer Babin." His face was a chorus of wrinkles, making him look a little like Gus, actually, and his scalp showed through his thin hair. Papaw Jack was old, but Mr. Babin was even older than that.

"Is there anyone I can call for you?" I asked. Mr. Babin shouldn't be alone. He was probably scared.

"My family lives out of town, but I can call them from the

hospital. You've been very helpful." He was having trouble talking and his face was very white. "But Gus . . ."

Gus pricked his ears up and howled again. The sirens were loud now. They had to be in front of the house.

"I'll go get them," I said.

Gus tried to dart between my legs as soon as I opened the gate, but I managed to snag his leash before he got too far. "No you don't," I told him. "Wait here."

A man and a woman got out of the ambulance. "We're back here!" I said. Gus began barking as I led them around to the backyard. "The dog is very nice," I assured them. The man had placed a big bag in the center of a stretcher, and he and the woman were both pushing the stretcher. "His hello is just really loud."

Gus nosed the bolt on the gate and it swung open. What a sneaky—and smart—dog! I grabbed his leash so the EMTs could get in, then steered Gus into the front yard and out of the way.

It wasn't long before they were wheeling Mr. Babin to the ambulance. "Someone will have to feed Gus," he said.

I looked down at Gus's sweet face. I knew exactly how it felt to be left behind.

"Don't worry," I told him. "You just get better. I'll take good care of Gus."

"Your grandpa is going to the hospital," the woman said. "Do you have someone to watch you?"

"He's not my grandpa," I said. "I'm just the neighbor who found him." I patted Gus on the back. "Well, Gus came and got me, actually." I had no doubt that Gus had opened that gate and gone looking for help.

The woman smiled. "Sounds like that's one smart dog."

"Yes, ma'am." I scratched Gus's ears. "You are a very good boy," I told him.

And then they were inside the ambulance and the sirens were on. Gus threw back his head and howled as they drove away, and I couldn't be sure if he was still just singing along with the sirens or if he was saying goodbye to Mr. Babin.

"He'll come back," I promised Gus when things finally went quiet. "Until then, I'm going to take good care of you."

And I wasn't going to abandon him in that tiny backyard either. I knew what lonely felt like, and I wasn't going to do that to Gus. Besides, it wasn't safe for him to escape and go wandering again. So even though I'd vowed not to be any trouble for Nana Pat and Papaw Jack, even though I didn't know a whole heck of a lot about dogs, for Gus, it was a risk I was willing to take. "You're coming home with me."

"Papaw Jack?" I hollered as I came through the back door. I'd put Gus in our backyard, which luckily had a sturdy gate he couldn't open, and he had quickly busied himself investigating every square inch. I figured that would keep him occupied for a little while at least.

Papaw Jack came shuffling out of the den. His eyes quickly scanned me head to toe, as if checking to see I wasn't hurt. He relaxed some. "You okay?" he asked.

"Yes." But now that I was home, I realized how shaky I was. My knees felt watery and my hands wobbled. "It's just . . ." And I told him about Gus asking for help and my finding Mr. Babin. Papaw Jack's eyes got wider and his eyebrows went up, up, up, until they'd almost completely hidden themselves in his thinning hair.

"Homer Babin okay?" he asked.

"I think he will be," I said. "Do you know him?"

"Not really. But I know who he is. He and his wife bought their house about the same time your Nana Pat and I bought this one."

Papaw Jack's face was grim and set. Maybe he was thinking about when he'd had his stroke. Nana Pat had found him out in his workshop. No one knew how long he'd been lying there.

He put his left arm around my shoulders and gave me a little squeeze. It steadied me a bit.

"There's something else." I tried to smile, but I was pretty sure it looked more like a grimace. "I told him I'd take care of Gus. His dog."

Papaw Jack didn't interrupt, just waited. He was a very good listener.

"So I brought Gus home. Uh, here." I pointed out the kitchen window.

Papaw Jack walked over to the window and peered out.

I shifted my weight from foot to foot and wiped my hands on my shorts. What if he said no? How could I leave Gus alone?

It was scary not knowing if or when your person was

going to return. I'd sat in a darkening apartment waiting for my mom. I wouldn't let Gus feel that too.

"Okay," Papaw Jack finally said.

My heart leaped. "Okay?" I was going to get to keep Gus? My brain told me it was just for a while, but my heart was too happy to listen. "He can really stay?"

Papaw Jack nodded, still staring out the window. "It's the right thing."

I squeaked a little. "Oh, thank you! Y'all won't even know he's here. I'll feed him and walk him and take such good care of him." I didn't know a whole lot about dogs. What I did know I'd learned from my dad's neighbor, but I figured making sure they were fed, walked, and loved was about all that was necessary. And I could do all that. I felt fizzy, like a cold drink that had been shaken up.

Papaw Jack glanced out the window. "Better clean him first."

I stood on my tiptoes to see out the window. Gus was stomping around in even more mud. I heard the words Papaw Jack didn't say: *before Nana Pat gets home.*

Bathing Gus in the backyard just meant adding to the mud, so I wiped his feet as best as I could and brought him inside. Papaw Jack patted Gus's head and retreated to his den.

"If you look like that when Nana Pat gets here, she definitely won't let you stay," I told Gus. And she might not let me stay either. "You are going to have to be on your very best behavior." I looked at the mud coat he was wearing. We'd have to work on that whole best-behavior thing. I led him toward the bathroom. "Let's get you a bath."

Apparently, Gus knew exactly what a bath was and was not a fan. He skidded to a stop and let out a terrific howl. It hurt my ears.

"Don't be like that," I said, trying to pull him into the bathroom. "It's just a bath."

He howled again.

"You did this to yourself," I reminded him.

And then I remembered that I still had half a cookie in my pocket. "If you go into this room," I said, omitting the word *bath*, "you can have a treat."

Gus looked at the cookie. Looked at the bathroom. Looked at me. I could see the moment he relented. He shoulders loosened a little bit, and then he let me take him into the bathroom. I shut the door behind us and rewarded him with a piece of cookie.

I took his collar off and turned on the water. Gus let out another ridiculous howl and tried to paw his way through the bathroom door. "If you keep that up, Nana Pat will not let you stay. Please be good."

I put the last of the cookie on the far edge of the tub. Gus glared at the water and glared at me. His eyes clearly called me a traitor. But he put his front paws in the water and leaned for the treat. I gave his behind a boost and got him all the way in the tub.

"See, that isn't so bad," I said.

He disagreed. Loudly. He howled as I poured water over him. The water turned brown. He howled some more. My ears rang.

At least he wasn't fighting me. He apparently had resigned

himself to the bath and sat obediently in the water, but he let me know in no uncertain terms just exactly how much he hated it.

I hadn't heard the bathroom door open over Gus's hollering, but suddenly Papaw Jack was there, slipping a pair of old earmuffs over my ears. It helped a little.

"Thanks!" I shouted. Papaw Jack got out of there quick. Smart man.

"You are going to look so handsome," I promised Gus as I poured shampoo over him. "Nana Pat will have to say yes." *Say yes, say yes, say yes,* my heart beat out.

I scrubbed and rinsed and scrubbed and rinsed again. Loose hair and clumps of dirt swirled down the drain. More of it stuck to the sides of the tub. "This is a crime scene," I muttered. I had to get this room spotless before Nana Pat came home.

"Good boy," I said for the hundredth time, trying to keep Gus calm. I reached for a towel, but it was too far away. "Stay," I told Gus.

Gus did not stay. As soon as I moved out of the way, Gus was out of the tub.

"Wait!"

Gus did not wait. Before I could get the towel over him, he shook, ears flapping wetly, entire body rolling, sending water across the floor, walls, ceiling, me. I'd already splashed water on my clothes, but now my legs and face and hair were wet. I tossed the towel over Gus and began drying him before he could do any more damage.

To my horror, the bathroom door opened and Nana Pat

stared in shock at the carnage. The bathtub was brown, everything was wet, and behind Nana Pat I could see Gus's muddy paw prints zigzagging from the kitchen and down the hallway, though it looked like Papaw Jack had been attempting to clean them up.

I forced a smile. "Surprise?"

CHAPTER FOUR

"Apparently you two cannot be trusted to stay out of trouble." Nana Pat stood in the middle of the kitchen with her hands planted firmly on her hips. She was still in her scrubs, and her face kept switching between annoyance and shock, like it couldn't decide which one to go with. At the moment, it had settled on annoyance.

I tried to look a little bit sorry, but I noticed Papaw Jack didn't bother. Nana Pat seemed to notice too.

"A dog?" she asked him. "What were you thinking?"

"It's the right thing." He spoke extra slow to make sure she heard every word.

Nana Pat opened her mouth, then snapped it shut without saying anything. That was new.

"Mr. Babin asked me to watch him," I said. I'd managed to tell Nana Pat most of the story.

Nana Pat's face softened. "I am proud of you for offering to help Mr. Babin. But a dog is a big responsibility." She emphasized *big*, making it clear that this particular dog was just big, period.

"He'll be so good," I promised. "You won't even know he's here!"

Nana Pat just laughed. "Honey, the entire neighborhood knows."

Gus was making an absolute racket. He was not the least bit thrilled about being shut out.

"He's lonely and scared," I said.

Gus bellowed again, a sound that was part howl, part bark, all sass. Then he pressed his nose against the door. I was pleased to see that he hadn't gotten muddy again. I could not leave that droopy-faced, sad-eyed dog outside alone all night.

"His entire world has been turned upside down." My words had a hard time getting past the stupid lump in my throat. "And this is a strange place to him."

Nana Pat blinked fast a few times, then her shoulders slumped and she threw up her hands. "I must be out of my mind," she muttered. "Let him in."

Gus practically tackled me as soon as I opened the door. I somehow managed not to fall over backward. I scratched his ears and rubbed his back. "Good boy." Then I leaned down and whispered in his ear. "If you want to stay inside, you're going to have to take it down several notches."

He answered by wagging his tail and sending Nana Pat's recipe box tumbling to the floor. I hurriedly scooped up the recipe cards and shoved them back in, but I was pretty sure they'd been organized and now decidedly were not.

"I better give him a tour," I said. Nana Pat stared at Gus

like she wasn't sure how he'd appeared in her very clean kitchen. Papaw Jack looked like he was trying not to grin.

"This is the kitchen," I told him.

"And you can stay out of it," Nana Pat added.

Gus blinked mournfully up at her, then ignored the rules and thoroughly inspected the room, sniffing at all the counters, underneath the table, and in two of the corners.

"Okay, this way." I took his collar and guided him out of the room. "The den is Papaw Jack's room," I said as we passed, "and I would also stay out of the living room if you know what's good for you." At least one of the lamps in there looked like it could be knocked over with a swipe of his tail, and the sofa was so clean even I was afraid to sit on it.

"You've seen the bathroom." I'd managed to get most of the dirt out of the tub after I'd put Gus out to both dry off and give Nana Pat some time to process.

"Now let's go see my room."

He followed me up the stairs, taking his own sweet time. He pushed through the door when I opened it and smelled everything, particularly my pile of dirty clothes.

"You're going to be very happy here." There it was again—saying aloud what I most wanted to be true. Was Gus already missing home? I hoped Mr. Babin was okay, that his family was on their way. No one should be alone when they were hurt. I felt a little guilty about how excited I was at having Gus here. But my room already felt cozier with him in it.

"Hmm," I said, realizing Gus didn't have a place to sleep. No way we were both fitting into my twin bed. "I guess I'd better make you a bed."

My room had two closets: one for my clothes and one for storage. Nana Pat kept extra blankets and boxes of Christmas decorations in that one. Gus followed me in and investigated while I rummaged around for something he could sleep on.

"Nope," I muttered, deciding against the handmade quilts. I could just imagine Nana Pat's face. I found a couple of faded comforters, one with a stain on it, and figured we were safe with those.

"Come on," I told Gus. He'd shoved his head into the back of the closet, and all I could see was his wagging tail. "Boy, you are even nosier than I am." I left him in the closet and carefully made him a pallet at the foot of my bed. I fluffed and tweaked it until it looked comfy.

Gus was still digging around in the closet. "Come on." I went back in and took him by the collar. "Get out of there."

He tugged a bit to stay, then finally backed out. I stared at the box he'd been sniffing—a large plastic bin with my mom's name written on it in black marker. Something warm fizzled in my stomach. "You are an excellent detective," I told Gus. I dragged the box out and put it next to my dresser.

I showed Gus his new bed. He sniffed all the sides and stomped through the middle. "This is your bed," I told him, squatting on the floor and patting the center of the blankets. "Want to try it out?"

Gus cocked his head. I wasn't sure how much he understood. "Sit."

He sank into a sit.

"Good boy!" I rubbed his ears. He seemed to really like that.

I left him to get used to his bed and opened the box with my mom's name on it. A row of yearbooks and a smaller box were lined up inside. I opened the smaller box.

It was full of loose pictures. Most of them were of my mom when she was in high school. She was laughing or smiling and making a goofy face in almost every single one of them. She looked so young.

But mixed in were a few of me when I was a baby. My eyes fell on one of them. Mom was lying on the couch in Nana Pat's living room. I was sleeping in her arms. My cheeks were pink and my mouth was slightly open and my hair was sticking straight up.

But it was my mom's face my eyes were drawn to. Because she was looking down at me and smiling. Her face looked like she was staring at the most wondrous thing she had ever seen.

I couldn't remember my mom ever looking at me like that. I slid the picture into the corner of the bulletin board with Dad's postcards.

Out of the corner of my eye, I saw Gus stand up and circle the bed. He spun one, two, three more times, then settled down.

I smiled. "Do you like it?"

He rested his head on his paws.

He liked it.

"Knock knock!" Nana Pat called up about an hour later. I shoved the yearbooks I'd been looking at under my bed. I'd found several pictures of my mom in there—in a cheerleading uniform in one, onstage in the school play in another—and seeing my mom's face, young, hopeful, different yet somehow the face I knew, made me feel all jumbled up.

Gus lumbered to his feet as the stairs creaked, and by the time Nana Pat poked her head in the door, his tail was beating out a frantic pattern on the bed. "How's it coming?" Nana Pat asked. If she noticed Gus's makeshift bed, she didn't say anything.

"We're fine," I said.

"And you have everything you need?"

My eyes found Gus. I couldn't help it. "Yes."

Gus, frustrated that she hadn't immediately patted him, complimented him, or fed him, edged closer to her and wagged his tail harder.

Nana Pat's eyes fell on the box next to my dresser, then snagged on the picture I'd just hung on the bulletin board. "I took that picture," she said. "Right after your first birthday party."

They'd sent me a birthday card with money for my last two birthdays, but they hadn't come to visit. I opened my mouth to ask why, but Nana Pat spoke before I could.

"Hand me your dirty clothes. I'm going to do a couple loads of laundry after dinner."

I hesitated. "I do my own laundry."

Nana Pat's eyebrows went up. "Do you?"

I pulled my shoulders back. "Since I was nine."

Nana Pat pursed her lips. She had deep creases around her mouth and smaller lines that fanned out around her eyes. I thought maybe since she was a nurse and all, she was just used to taking care of people. (I'd overheard Mom say once that Nana Pat was used to bossing people.) But as thoroughly as I examined her face, as much as I tried to use all that I had learned about reading expressions from mystery novels, I had no idea what she was thinking.

I realized that I was just as much of a mystery to Nana Pat as she was to me. We weren't complete strangers, but we were really only family by blood. We'd missed a lot of knowing each other. Maybe Nana Pat was just as unsure as I was.

Gus would be ignored no longer. He sniffed Nana Pat's shoes, then her knees, and finally looked up at her expectantly. Nana Pat reached down and scratched one of his floppy ears. Her hand came back covered in slobber. She looked at it in horror, glanced around helplessly for a second, then sighed and held her hand a little way away from her body.

"Well, you are welcome to continue to do your own laundry, but I will need to give you a lesson on using my washer and dryer. I am very particular." She softened the words with a small smile. "And dinner's ready."

Gus's ears twitched. He obviously knew the word *dinner*.

"Okay, thanks."

She turned and headed back downstairs, and Gus and I followed.

It was comical following a bloodhound downhill. Gus waddled and galumphed, clumsy and lumbering, and stepped on one of his ears once he got to the bottom of the stairs.

Gus headed straight for the kitchen, nose in the air as he hunted for Nana Pat's meatloaf.

"Nope. You'd better stay in that hallway," she said. Papaw Jack had just come into the kitchen, and he looked up in surprise.

"Not you." Nana Pat chuckled. "The dog."

Papaw Jack sat at the table and Nana Pat used the extra kitchen chair to block the doorway from the hall into the kitchen. Gus lay down on the floor with a huff.

I'd never had a dog before, so I didn't know if all dogs were so expressive or if that was just Gus. But I was learning quick that he had quite the personality.

Papaw Jack ate with his left hand, which was hard for him, and he had to eat slow since one side of his face drooped a little. Nana Pat ate quickly and efficiently. She fussed and bossed and blustered, and if Papaw Jack was going to add something to the conversation, he sure didn't get the chance.

"I'm off tomorrow but I'll check on Mr. Babin when I go in Thursday," Nana Pat said.

"Thank you," I said.

Gus started whining. I wasn't yet fluent in Gus, but I thought it probably meant *No fair*.

"Stay in the hallway, buddy." I took another bite of meatloaf. It was really good, for something called meatloaf.

Gus pushed the chair blocking the hallway out of the way with his big body and went to the back door. He whined again, then scratched on the door.

"I think he needs to go out." Mr. Babin must have trained Gus very well. I stood up and went around the left side of the table toward the door. Meanwhile, Gus went around the right side and would have eaten my meatloaf if Nana Pat hadn't reached out and stopped him just in time.

I quickly covered my grin with my hand. Nana Pat looked absolutely over it. Papaw Jack laughed.

"That's one smart dog," he said.

Yes, he was. And it looked like he had a little thief in him.

I shook my finger at Gus. "That was not very nice," I told him. "You'll get your dinner in just a minute, and I can promise you I won't try to steal even a single bite." I opened the back door. He didn't budge. "You were fibbing?" I asked him. He turned and headed back toward the kitchen table. "Oh no you don't." I took him by the collar and steered him up the stairs. I hated to shut him in my room, but I wasn't sure what Nana Pat would do if he stole food out of her kitchen.

I spent the rest of dinner listening to Gus pitch a fit and Nana Pat try to talk over him, pretending that Gus wasn't bellowing like cattle from the top floor. Papaw Jack looked wildly pleased at the racket. It took a special person to appreciate a bloodhound's singing. But apparently Papaw Jack did.

"I saw that old lady next door glaring at your garden today," I said.

"Her name is Edna Gill, and she glares at everything," Nana Pat said.

"She looks a bit dodgy—might be a tomato thief."

Papaw Jack coughed and took a drink of his water.

"Edna Gill is not stealing my tomatoes." Nana Pat gave me a good once-over. "You're nosy, aren't you? Not unlike Edna Gill."

"I prefer *curious*. All great detectives are." The best detectives noticed what other people didn't. Besides, Nana Pat couldn't judge—she was just as nosy as I was. She called it a prayer chain, but from what I could tell, it was just an excuse for her and her friends to call each other and gossip.

"Did you get everything unpacked?" Nana Pat asked.

"Pretty much. But I can't find my pink Converse, and I know I packed them."

"You're supposed to pray to Saint Anthony. Whenever I've lost something, I just repeat the prayer three times and it turns up."

I'd never heard of Saint Anthony. "Did you pray to Saint Anthony for my mom?"

"What?" Her voice was a little sharper than usual.

"My mom. Maybe Saint Anthony can help find her."

Nana Pat's eyes were shiny as she gathered up her silverware and plate. "Help me clean the kitchen."

Nana Pat had been dodging talking about Mom every bit as much as Dad had. I was getting sick of it. But I didn't push. I was afraid if I made her mad, she'd send me away. And I didn't have anywhere else to go.

I took my plate to the sink. Gus barked. I rinsed my plate

and put it in the dishwasher. Gus howled. I hid a piece of meatloaf in a napkin when no one was looking and shoved it into my pocket. Gus kicked the bedroom door and basically yodeled.

Nana Pat threw down her dish towel. "Go look after that dog before he destroys my house."

Gus quieted as I climbed the stairs, then almost knocked me down as I opened the bedroom door.

"You are very demanding," I said, rubbing his ears. He sniffed at the meatloaf squirreled away in my pocket. "That's for later."

I looked over his shoulder. Blinked. Had to walk inside for a closer look.

Soggy scraps of cardboard were scattered across my room. He'd shredded and chewed one of my empty cardboard packing boxes.

"You are too old to throw tantrums," I told him. I frowned and put my hands on my hips, mimicking Nana Pat.

Gus did not appear intimidated—or sorry. He just looked up at me and wagged his tail.

And then I saw the mess next to my bed. He'd knocked a glass of water and a stack of books off the nightstand. "You didn't." I picked up the books, which were soaking wet and ruined. The cover of *Murder on the Orient Express* had been torn off.

These books were secondhand, they were musty and stained, but they were some of the few things that were mine. I whirled on Gus, close to tears. "Bad dog!"

His tail drooped a little.

I shook the books at him. "These are not yours. That was very bad!" I was yelling louder than was necessary, and I knew it. I threw the books on the floor and sat on my bed. "You are ungrateful. Maybe you should sleep outside."

Gus sat down in front of me and batted my knee lightly with his paw. Shame flushed through me. "I didn't mean that," I whispered. I wasn't even really mad at him. I was frustrated with Nana Pat and angry with my parents. Maybe Gus had the right idea.

I grabbed another empty packing box and ripped off a flap. "I'm mad," I admitted. Gus cocked his head, listening. I tore off another flap. "I hate secrets, and silence, and being treated like a baby!" I punctuated my words by destroying the box. Gus, eager to be helpful, began tearing up the cardboard I dropped. I growled and grunted and shredded the box.

When I was done, I sank to the floor. Gus rolled in the shredded box. "You're right," I told Gus. "I'm sorry I thought you were just being dramatic with all the howling and destruction. I actually do feel a little better."

Gus rolled over and grinned at me. A soggy piece of cardboard stuck to his lower lip.

"And I'm sorry I fussed at you." I put my hand on his head. "You're allowed to be sad and confused. But maybe don't tear up any more of my books, please?" I would do a better job keeping trouble out of his way. "But I would never abandon you," I told him. "No matter how bad you messed up." I didn't know how much he understood, but I thought it was important for me to say it.

He shoved his head into my lap. Just like that, I was forgiven.

But as easy as it was to have Gus's love, I vowed to earn it—and return it. "You hungry?"

Gus ran down the stairs. Well, maybe *ran* was too generous a word. He sort of trotted and wobbled and jiggled his way down the steps. It didn't completely erase my frustration at Nana Pat for not wanting to talk about Mom, but it helped a little.

I took him into the laundry room, where I'd put food and water bowls. We were going to have to get real dog food tomorrow. Tonight, Nana Pat had made Gus some rice and beef broth. "Don't get used to this," I told him, putting down his food. I placed the bite of meatloaf in the center.

Gus sounded like a garbage disposal as he ate, and his bowl was soon empty. "You didn't even chew it," I fussed. "I took the trouble of sneaking that meatloaf out. The least you could do was taste it."

He bent down to drink water. His long ears floated in the bowl. He drank very loudly, water splashing all around the bowl and onto the wall. When he finished and lifted his head, water and drool ran out of the sides of his mouth. I put my hands up. I knew what was coming. Still, when he shook off, I got splattered.

"Gross, Gus," I whined.

He wagged his tail, not caring in the least that I had drool and water and maybe a couple of pieces of soggy food on me. I squatted down beside him. "I'm so glad you're here, even if I can't keep you forever."

He wiped his mouth on my shirt. I was pretty sure that meant he was happy too.

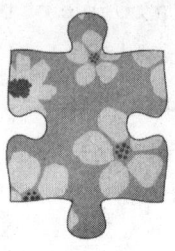

CHAPTER FIVE

Nana Pat and Papaw Jack's house was quiet at night, which made it easier for those super-loud questions to find me. Where was Mom? Did she miss me?

What had I done wrong?

Loneliness sat on my chest and made it hard to breathe. I thought maybe Gus felt some of that loneliness too. He paced the room and looked at the door.

I knew exactly what it felt like to spend the night in a strange place.

I pulled my pillow and blanket off my bed and made myself a little nest next to Gus's blanket. I patted the space beside me. "Want to sit?"

He looked at the door one more time before coming to sit in front of me. I rubbed his chest. "I'll tell you a story."

I kept petting Gus, keeping my voice calm as I told him all the best parts of *Death on the Nile*. He seemed to be listening. Then his eyes started to droop a bit. He swayed a little. I smiled and kept talking. Finally, he lay down on his bed.

I curled up next to him and continued the story. He didn't

seem nearly as shocked by the ending as I had been, but he was a detective dog, so maybe he'd figured it out.

Gus was asleep by the time I ran out of story. My heart tugged in his direction as I looked at his wrinkled face. And then Gus started snoring.

It wasn't a cute little dog snore either. He snored like a chain saw. But even that wasn't enough to run me out of the nest I'd made on the floor next to him. I grinned into my pillow and pulled the blanket up around my shoulders, and instead of lying awake for hours like I usually did, I drifted off on a tide of Gus snores and didn't wake up until the sun threw sparkles across my bedroom floor.

Not that it was the sparkles that woke me up. It was Gus, snuffling at my ear, that did the trick. I smiled and blinked awake. "Good morning."

Gus's tail thumped on the floor. I put my hands over my face as he inspected my hair.

"No breakfast in there," I told him. I stood up and stretched. "I bet you have to go out, don't you?"

I threw on some clothes and took him downstairs.

The back door opened as we stepped into the kitchen, and Nana Pat pushed through carrying a basket full of vegetables.

Gus gave a very loud bark.

"Ahhh!" Nana Pat shouted. She dropped the basket, and vegetables went rolling across the kitchen floor.

Gus darted forward and snagged a tomato before I could stop him.

"It's bad enough that that dog nearly gave me a heart

attack," Nana Pat fussed. "But now he's stealing my tomatoes!"

Gus and I played chase around the kitchen. Every time I thought I had him, he would dart just out of reach. He was faster than he looked. I could have sworn he was smirking at me, though it was hard to tell around the tomato. I finally got him cornered and managed to wrestle the tomato away from him. It had gotten mostly squished in the process. I held it out to Nana Pat.

"Well, I don't want it now," she said. She pointed to the trash can and I tossed it in.

I opened the back door and Gus galloped out into the morning.

I really needed Gus to be a good dog so Nana Pat wouldn't send him away. I knew I wasn't going to get to keep him forever, but he was mine for right now at least, and I couldn't stand the thought of losing him already.

"Can I take Gus to the park?"

Nana Pat seemed relieved. "Absolutely. And wear him out before you bring him back."

So, after we'd had breakfast and Nana Pat had lectured me on being safe and going straight to the park and straight back, we headed out the front door.

I gripped his leash firmly in my fist. "Let's find adventure."

Gus set off at a trot, ears swaying.

The trot didn't last long. He sniffed a mailbox. He ambled down the sidewalk. He smelled the grass, and a tree, and treated a plastic bag with the deepest suspicion.

"We're not going to make it to the park until next week at this rate," I muttered, but I didn't mind going slow.

But when we finally did make it to the park, Gus refused to go in. "You want to keep walking?"

I'd told Nana Pat we wouldn't go anywhere else, but Gus tugged at the leash, and I wasn't going to tell him no. We just wouldn't go very far.

Gus walked faster now, not sniffing, and when he took a right at the corner, I knew exactly where he was going. My heart felt very fragile.

Soon we were standing in front of 208 Giselle Street. "You miss home, don't you, buddy?"

I understood.

Gus led me to the backyard. I let us in and dropped the leash as he bounded into the yard. Gus examined the spot where Mr. Babin had fallen, then ran up the steps.

"Be careful!" I told him, but he jumped over the busted one in the middle. He sniffed the full length of the back porch, then ran up and scratched at the back door.

"Oh, buddy, he's not home. I'm so sorry." But while the head could be reasoned with, the heart was soft and stubborn. Gus pawed at the door again.

I knew what it was like to wait for someone who never came home. The last time I'd seen Mom, she'd been getting into her car to head to work. I hadn't even waved goodbye as I'd climbed onto the school bus. I hadn't known I might not ever see her again.

It had been a normal day. I'd spent my lunch reading in the

school library. Sometimes I ate in the cafeteria. I was friendly enough with some of the kids in class, but often they talked about sleepovers Mom never let me go to or shows I hadn't watched, and it was just nicer to escape all that by spending some time with problems that were solved by the last page. I'd come home to an empty house like I usually did. Done my homework. Texted Mom. She hadn't answered.

I'd sat at the dining table and worked on a puzzle. The apartment grew darker. Mom still didn't come home.

I'd jumped when someone knocked on the door. I knew not to open it. It was the first thing Mom had told me when she'd started leaving me at home alone.

"Glory, it's Dad!" His deep rumble came through the door.

I peered through the peephole. It really was Dad. I opened the door.

Dad stepped inside. He wore faded blue jeans, scuffed boots, and an old Harley-Davidson T-shirt. His hair was a mess of floppy brown curls, and they gave off the same laid-back vibe. "Hey, Glory Bee." He swept me up in a hug, but not before I saw that his forehead was furrowed. I knew something was up then. My dad never worried.

"Hey, Dad. What are you doing here?" He lived in Lafayette. I never saw him during the week.

"Your mom texted me. She went away for a little while. So you're coming to stay with me."

"Went where?" I asked, a little panicked. We were getting evicted. She couldn't just leave. We had to pack.

"Your mom needs a vacation. Don't you want to stay with me?"

The deep breath I took to steady my heart did not help. "I do. But I have school." And Dad lived forty-five minutes away.

He sighed and rubbed the back of his neck. "I forgot."

I loved my dad, but sometimes I believed that anything not right in front of his face ceased to exist for him. How could he not know I had school?

He looked worried and uncomfortable, which made him look like he was wearing someone else's clothes. "Guess we can stay here for a while."

"Not long. They're evicting us."

Dad's face was a storm cloud now.

"Where is Mom really?" I asked. She wouldn't have just taken off, would she?

Dad stood up straighter. "Like I said, on vacation. Are you hungry? I'm starving."

I nodded. It was clear Dad wasn't going to tell me anything. I was going to have to solve this mystery by myself.

I'd talked Dad into letting me stay at home while he went to pick up dinner. I waited until I was sure he was gone before running into Mom's room.

All of her clothes were gone. Her shoes. The dusty box of pictures she kept under her bed. People on vacation didn't pack that much stuff. My fingers felt numb.

I went into the kitchen. The eviction notice and a large stack of unpaid bills sat near the coffeepot.

I opened the cabinets. Most of the dishes were still there, but Mom's favorite mug was gone.

I called her phone.

"The number you have dialed is no longer in service."

I hung up.

I barely ate any of the dinner Dad brought home. He didn't seem to notice.

After Dad had fallen asleep on the couch watching TV, I slipped his phone off the coffee table and tiptoed into the kitchen. He didn't lock his phone, so opening his text messages was easy. I knew it was wrong, but I'd read enough mysteries to know there were always clues. And sometimes you had to dance on the line between right and wrong to find them.

The last text message my mom had sent my dad was only two words: *Your turn.*

And then Dad hadn't really wanted his turn either, because he'd sent me to Nana Pat and Papaw Jack.

I sat on the top step of Mr. Babin's porch and leaned my head against the weathered railing. I didn't know how I could make Gus understand that it wasn't his fault. Mr. Babin hadn't wanted to leave him. He'd thought about Gus even before anything else.

Gus stopped pawing at the door, finally realizing no one was going to open it. He sank down beside me. I knew he couldn't understand everything I was saying, but I was going to give him the truth. He deserved it.

"He didn't abandon you," I said. "He got hurt, remember? And he had to go to the hospital. Nana Pat said she's going to check on him. But he's going to be fine, and he's going to come home, and y'all are going to be so happy again."

And Gus happy would make me happy. Even if letting him go would hurt.

"While he's gone, we are going to have a lot of fun."

Gus nudged me with his nose. I threw my arm over him and leaned my head against his side. I could hear his heart beat. He had a very strong heart.

"You just had to make sure, didn't you?" I sat up straight. "Gus, you're a genius."

Dad had stayed with me in our apartment for a few days, long enough for me to pack and finish enough of the sixth grade. Mom hadn't called or texted again. But maybe she'd told someone at work where she was going. Maybe she'd even given them an address so they could mail her paycheck!

I took out my phone and called Mom's work. It only rang twice.

"Jimmy's Grill."

I froze.

"Hello?"

"Hi." My voice cracked. "Is Layla St. Romain there?"

"Layla St. Romain doesn't work here."

So, she really had left town. "Have you talked to her recently?"

"Who is this?"

"Glory St. Romain. Her daughter."

When the woman spoke again, she didn't sound so rushed. "How old are you, Glory?"

I didn't see why that mattered, but I told her anyway. "Twelve."

The woman's sigh had weight. "Layla was let go about six months ago. I haven't seen her since."

She'd been fired? Six whole months ago?

"Glory?"

"Okay thank you bye." I hung up and put the phone out of my reach, like this was somehow its fault.

Why hadn't Mom told me she'd gotten fired? And she hadn't just not told me—she'd pretended it never happened. She apologized for working late and complained about her manager, the same manager she'd complained about for the past year.

I couldn't decide if Mom was good at hiding the truth or just kept losing track of it.

But I hadn't once suspected. Some detective I was.

One of the good things about having a dog was that you couldn't sit around feeling sorry for yourself. I filled the bowl next to the house with water from the hose and waited while Gus drank. I'd learned to stay far enough away that his shaking shower of slobber didn't land on me. I let him sniff for a little while more in his yard, then I picked up his leash.

"Let's go to the park."

And this time he followed me.

It felt good to step into the shade of the park. Gus and I were the only ones there again. I held on to his leash but let him go where he wanted. He tugged me toward the back of the park. A large patch of grass was surrounded on three sides by trees and bushes. They'd gotten thick and unruly. Gus liked that. He pushed and pulled his way into every space, and once he startled a squirrel. I thought I was done for then, but he didn't even chase after it, just put his nose down and went to sniffing again.

Then he seemed to get on the trail of something. He snorted, then lifted his head and listened. He gave a quiet bark and started pulling me.

"Where are we headed?" He strained against the leash, definitely on the trail of something.

And then we were in the bushes. Branches and leaves poked me in the face, hit me across the mouth. "Hey. You need to stop."

He did not stop.

I managed to yank him to a halt just before a pointy branch almost took out my right eye. "Where—"

The trees and bushes opened up a bit, revealing two large boys standing threateningly close to a rather small boy. Gus and I stayed out of sight. "This is our fort," one of the bigger boys told the smaller one.

I looked around. I didn't see a fort, but I did see a huge weeping willow. I imagined that sitting against its trunk would be like being surrounded by long green curtains.

The small boy was clutching a red stuffed crab. "My brother said—"

"Your brother isn't here," the other boy said.

It did not take a detective to know that the bigger boys were not friends with the little guy. They were, in fact, large bullies that I would quite happily take down a peg or two.

"Hey, Gus, do you want a bath?"

Gus jerked his head around to look at me, then gave an extremely loud (and honestly quite frightening) bark.

The boys jumped.

Gus and I stepped out of our hiding spot. "I believe you need a bath, Gus," I whispered. "You stink."

This time Gus's bark of protestation was even louder.

The big boys looked afraid, and the little boy looked absolutely petrified. I hated that I was scaring him, but there was nothing for it.

I pretended to struggle with Gus's leash, and Gus, to his credit, really leaned into the role. He lunged forward, and I hoped neither one of them noticed how happily his tail was wagging. "I may not be able to hold him back much longer!" I shouted. "Bath," I said again under my breath.

Gus let out a mournful bay. He still hadn't forgiven me for his last bath. Because the boys could not speak bloodhound, and sass sounded a lot like anger, the bigger boys took off.

The smaller boy backed up against a tree. His dark hair was sticking up in the back and plastered to his forehead in the front. His glasses were held on by a rubber strap that went all the way around his head, making them look more like goggles. He had dirt on his legs and shorts, and I hoped it was from playing rather than from having been knocked down.

"He won't hurt you," I said as soon as the bullies were out of earshot. "He's just really loud."

"Are you s-s-s-sure?" he asked.

I sank to the ground and held Gus's leash even tighter. "I promise." Gus glanced at me and, after realizing I didn't intend to spring water and shampoo on him any time soon, sank into a sit. "You can pet him if you want."

The boy's eyes were round, and I was fairly certain that a strong wind would blow him over, but he came closer. He was ten times braver than either of those bullies. Gus sat very still as the boy reached out and patted his head. A tentative smile crept across his face.

"See? I was just making him bark to scare off those other boys."

"Sebastian!"

The boy jumped. A girl charged through the bushes. She looked to be about my age and was tall and skinny, all knees and elbows and angles. If Gus hadn't scared the bigger boys away, I was pretty sure her expression would have. A younger girl, tiny with curly hair, ran behind her.

"What have I told you about running off?" the older girl asked.

"Sorry!" Sebastian squeaked.

"You found a puppy!" the little girl squealed.

She wasn't afraid. She marched straight up to Gus. "I'm Lydie." She threw her arms around his neck. He drooled a bit in her hair.

"The dog saved me," Sebastian said.

I grinned. "That's giving Gus a lot of credit. He just barked and ran a couple of older kids off."

The girl took me and Gus in for a minute before focusing back on the boy. "Tate and Scotty?"

Sebastian nodded, then stepped closer to Gus and began petting him with both hands.

Gus was comforting like that.

"I'm Glory, by the way."

The girl looked me and Gus over again, her expression both careful and curious, like the way Mom sometimes looked when she was trying to decide if we were going to be able to afford all the groceries in the cart. We must have passed the test, because she finally gave a curt nod. "I'm Rosemary." She pointed at the little boy and girl, who were still petting Gus. "My little brother and sister. Thank you for your help."

"I can't stand bullies."

Rosemary's jaw tightened. "You would think they would have better things to do."

"They might be busy washing out their shorts right now." I grinned. "Gus gave them a good scare."

Rosemary blinked. Then she cackled. There was no other word for it. She threw back her head and shrieked with laughter.

That kind of laughter was contagious. I doubled over, laughing hard enough that I snorted, which made both of us laugh harder. Eventually even Sebastian and Lydie started giggling. Gus cocked his head and gave all four of us a weary stare, as if humans were beyond comprehension.

Rosemary sighed and wiped her eyes, then took Sebastian's hand. "We should get home."

"Awww," Lydie whined. "Can't we play with Gus a little longer?"

Rosemary blushed. "Gus might not want to play."

Gus needed to get all his energy out before we went back to Nana Pat's. "It's fine with me," I said. "We were just hanging out in the park."

"For a little while, then," Rosemary told her sister.

Lydie bounced up and down and clapped. Sebastian smiled timidly. We followed Rosemary down to a path through the bushes.

"Couldn't have used the path?" I muttered to Gus.

"So did you just move here?" Rosemary asked. "I don't think I've seen you at school."

"I'm staying with my grandparents for the summer." I didn't elaborate on the reason why.

"Fun. I wish my parents would let me go visit mine all by myself for the summer. When I go, all my brothers and sisters have to come with me."

We stepped back into the park and sat on the bench where I'd first met Gus. Lydie and Sebastian sank to the grass in front of him.

"How many siblings do you have?" I asked.

"Four."

"Four!" I couldn't imagine a house filled with that many people. "I'm an only child."

"Lucky," Rosemary said. "My other brother and sister get to do whatever they want while I corral the two littles."

Rosemary looked thoroughly put out by it, but I thought it sounded wonderful. I'd been surrounded by quiet lately, the kind of quiet that had mass. Enough to smother a person.

"And the littles have a tendency to break things if they get cooped up in the house for too long."

"The last few rainy days must have been fun," I said.

She gave me a pitiful look. "You have no idea. They broke a vase and several dishes. And then Lydie got into my older sister's makeup. It was complete carnage."

"Sounds like Lydie and Gus would get along famously. He is also known for carnage." And that was only in the last twenty-four hours I'd known him.

"Your dog is a hit," Rosemary said. Sebastian's face had lost all trace of fear, and Lydie was making Gus a flower crown.

"He's only my dog for a little while," I told her. "I'm watching him while his owner is in the hospital."

"So you're babysitting this summer too!" And she smiled at me.

I smiled back.

Fifteen minutes later, Gus was also wearing a flower necklace. "I'd better go," I said. I still wasn't sure how likely Nana Pat would be to call the cops if I was five minutes late. "We'll be back, though. Gus likes this park."

Rosemary smiled. "I'm sure Lydie and Sebastian will be thrilled." Both were hugging Gus goodbye. "We haven't hung out here much since they got rid of the swings, but Gus is a very good babysitter, and I wouldn't mind hanging out with someone my own age for a change." She looked a little shy when she said it.

"Same," I said, that fizzy feeling returning.

We grinned at each other.

I waved at the little kids and led Gus out of the park and back onto the sidewalk. I felt much lighter on the walk back.

CHAPTER SIX

Nana Pat called me from the hospital on Thursday.

"I have someone who wants to talk to you," she said.

"Hello?" A man's voice came through the phone. "This is Homer Babin."

He sounded better than the last time I'd talked to him. Was he getting out of the hospital already? I felt just awful about hoping they'd keep him a little while longer, but I wanted more time with Gus. We were just getting to know each other. "Hi, Mr. Babin!" I tried to brighten up my worry. "How are you feeling?"

"I've been better," he admitted. "I'm having surgery tomorrow, so it's going to be a while before I get to go home."

"I'm sorry." And I was. I was sorry Mr. Babin was hurt. I was sorry Gus missed him. But I was not sorry that Gus got to stay.

"Your grandma told me Gus is staying at your house. Thank you so much for keeping him company."

"He's keeping me company too." I reached over to pat Gus's head. He was drooling a little. He did that pretty often.

"I hope he's behaving." Mr. Babin sounded a tad doubtful.

"He is a very good boy."

Mr. Babin laughed. "He is. But he also has a nose for trouble. I'm so glad Gus has someone young to run around with for a change. I haven't exactly been very fair to him lately."

Gus had always looked well loved to me.

"My wife died two years ago. Funny how time doesn't exactly play by the rules. When a person is gone, it feels like last week and a hundred years ago all at the same time."

I knew exactly what he meant. The last time I saw my mom felt like only yesterday and also a very long time ago.

"I was lonely, so I went down to the pound. I couldn't believe it when I saw Gus. He's a purebred bloodhound. The family who'd dropped him at the pound had said he was just too much—too big, too loud, too stubborn."

Gus was all of those things, but I could not believe someone would want to get rid of him. Gus must have been so sad. He wouldn't have understood that he hadn't done anything wrong.

I leaned against Gus to make sure he knew he wasn't alone now.

"And he is a handful," Mr. Babin said.

"I believe Nana Pat would agree with you."

"A big dog like that, smart as he is, needs exercise and adventure. His first family hadn't wanted to give him those things. I had this wild idea that I was going to train him to follow trails. Bloodhound noses can be used as evidence in court, you know?"

I had not known. He really was a detective dog!

"But I never ended up even trying. Even before this broken leg, I wasn't able to get around that much. It wasn't fair, taking this big dog full of wanderlust and trying to make him be content just sitting by my chair. He needed open spaces."

"You gave him a home."

"And he was good company."

He really was. "We've been taking walks and going to the park. He even protected a boy from bullies the other day," I told him.

"I'm glad to hear that. Very glad. Listen to me, going on and on."

I thought maybe Mr. Babin was still a little lonely.

"Do you want to talk to Gus?" I asked. I put the phone on speaker. "Say hi to Mr. Babin, Gus."

"Hi, buddy." Mr. Babin's voice filled my room. Gus looked at the phone and cocked his head.

"He's listening," I said.

"You be very good," Mr. Babin told him.

Gus looked around, like he expected Mr. Babin to be standing in the corner. He looked back at the phone and cocked his head again.

"I miss you so much."

Gus pawed my leg. "He's trying to pat the phone," I said, laughing a little. "I think that means he misses you too."

"I'm going to rest now," Mr. Babin said, and he sounded tired. "Thanks again, Glory. I'd be worried sick about him if it weren't for you."

"You don't have to worry about him at all," I told him. "You just get better."

"Bye now." And he hung up the phone.

I put my forehead to Gus's and scratched his ears. "Court evidence, huh?" A piece of a puzzle snapped into place. What if I trained Gus to track? How happy would Mr. Babin be when he got out of the hospital and I could show him what Gus could do? How happy would Gus be if I let him do what he was born to do?

After about ten minutes of research on my phone, I stood up. "Gus, I think it's time that we went to the library."

The Sweet Olive Library was a very old building tucked behind shade trees. It was a pretty long walk from Nana Pat and Papaw Jack's, but Gus didn't mind walking. I think he liked the attention. Everyone we met asked what kind of dog he was, or if they could pet him, or just said hello. I noticed that most people became their best selves when they were with dogs.

Gus was panting by the time we got to the library. It was cloudy, but the air was thick and damp; it felt like breathing through a wet sponge.

The glass doors slid open as Gus and I walked up, and gloriously cold air escaped. Funny how I could smell the library without even stepping inside. It reminded me of summers with my mom when I was little. The library was one of the places we could go that didn't cost anything. Mom would use the free internet and I'd read books.

She never let me check out the books, though, because she never knew when she could bring me back. But once I started school, I could check out all the books from the school library. I spent a lot of my free time there. Every time we moved apartments, I'd have to switch schools. Being a new kid was hard, but the library always felt safe. And I never once met a mean librarian. The one at my last school introduced me to Agatha Christie. Once I'd read all the mysteries she had in the library, she'd even brought me some of her own books from home.

They'd kept me company when Mom was out working.

"You can't bring your dog in here."

I jerked my head up. The woman behind the counter had gray hair and glasses and a kind face, even if she was fussing at me a little bit.

"Oh. Okay." I turned around and went back outside. An empty bench sat underneath some shade trees right outside a large bank of windows. If I tied Gus's leash to the bench, I could still see him from inside. "Do you think you'll be okay for just a few minutes?" I asked him.

He rolled his mournful eyes at me. I wasn't sure if he was offended at the question or dismayed at the idea he would have to stay outside by himself.

I tied his leash around the arm of the bench. "I'll be superfast," I promised. I didn't want to leave him alone, but now that I was here, I didn't want to leave without books either.

I walked away. Gus tugged forward and whimpered when he got as far as the leash would go. "Stay," I told him. "I will be right back."

I hurried inside.

The librarian smiled at me. "Can I help you?"

"I'm looking for books on bloodhounds."

Her eyes darted to the window, and mine followed. Gus was peering inside, his breath fogging up the glass. The librarian seemed torn between annoyance that he was getting her window dirty and joy at that wrinkly face.

Gus seemed to have that effect on a lot of people. Including Nana Pat.

The librarian settled behind her computer and typed. "Fiction?"

"No." My face grew warm, and I lowered my voice, even though what I said next wasn't all that embarrassing or a secret. "I'm going to train him to track and need to know how."

"Oh! Okay. Well, let's see." She scrolled and then wrote a couple of things down on a small piece of paper. Then she came around the counter.

"Follow me. I'm Ms. Caroline."

"Glory."

"What a lovely name."

I'd always thought so too.

Ms. Caroline took me over to a shelf toward the back of the library. "Right here." She pointed to several books, then handed me the paper with numbers on it. "I'll let you look. I'll be up front if you need me."

I pulled a book down and began flipping through it. I put it aside and took down another one. I found one book on tracking and one book on mantrailing. I even found a whole book just on bloodhounds and how to take care of them. I added that one to my stack. They had a lot more books on a lot more different kinds of dogs, but as much as I wanted to flip through them, Gus was waiting on me. I headed back up front.

I became aware of noise. Everyone was looking toward the front door and laughing. I had a very bad feeling. I peered around the group of adults.

Gus had pulled the bench away from the window and around the corner and was sitting in front of the automatic door, which had registered his presence and opened dutifully. I had no doubt that if the bench hadn't snagged on the corner of the building, Gus would have pulled the entire thing inside.

He was wet. I realized then that the clouds had finally gotten too heavy. It was raining.

"I'm sorry," I told Ms. Caroline, who, rather than looking angry, looked like this was the best thing she'd seen all day. I lowered my voice. "We walked here. Is there anywhere we can hang out until it stops?" I was not leaving Gus outside alone in the rain.

She frowned, then sighed. "All right, take him around the back."

I put my books on the counter and ran outside.

Gus thumped his tail and gave me a very wet kiss when I leaned down and scratched his ears. "You are very impatient,"

I told him, but I couldn't be mad. The fact that he missed me and wanted to be with me made me feel special.

I untied him and pulled the bench close to where it had been. Now we were both wet. We hurried around the building. Ms. Caroline was standing just inside the back door.

"He'll have to be quiet," she said. She opened another door just inside. "This is my office. Stay right here."

"Thank you."

She handed me the books I'd left on the counter. "To keep you busy." She shut the door behind her.

Ms. Caroline's office was a little messy. Stacks of books and papers were everywhere. It was most definitely not dog friendly.

"Don't touch anything," I told Gus.

But he was in a new place, so that meant sniffing. I winced as his tail knocked over a small stack of books.

I opened up the bloodhound book and started reading.

"Did you know that one of the most famous bloodhounds looked just like you? He was red and his name was Nick Carter. He had over six hundred fifty finds, and once he even followed a trail for fifty-five miles!"

I showed Gus the picture. He didn't seem all that impressed.

"No pressure, though," I assured him.

The rain was loud on the roof now, a sudden downpour that made me glad we hadn't gotten caught walking home.

I read. Gus sniffed. I learned about how a bloodhound's nose worked. Gus stuck his in all of Ms. Caroline's stuff.

He must have smelled something interesting, because he

pushed his rather large body between two bookshelves. They wobbled.

"Careful," I told him.

He ignored me. I'd started wondering if his ears worked less when his nose was working more.

He knocked another stack of books over. "Gus," I hissed. I tried to grab his collar, but most of his body was hidden. Just his behind and tail stuck out.

"Get out of there," I said. "You are going to get us in so much trouble."

The thought of trouble didn't seem to bother Gus in the least. When he was on a clue, getting to the bottom of it was all that mattered.

He began scooting out, toppling a stack of folders as he did. I scooped them back up, hoping they hadn't been in any special order.

Gus finally emerged, a purple-and-gold sweater in his mouth.

"No. That is not yours. Drop it."

He bucked. He wanted me to chase him.

"We are not doing that in here."

He shook his head back and forth, sweater swinging.

"Detectives are supposed to solve crimes, not commit them."

Ms. Caroline opened the door. Her eyes widened. "My sweater!"

"I am so sorry!" I managed to get ahold of it, but Gus was not letting go.

"Good boy!" Ms. Caroline said.

I wasn't sure I'd heard her clearly.

She smiled. "I've been looking for that sweater for a month. Where did he find it?"

I pointed to the stacks. "Back there."

She looked embarrassed. "I have got to straighten this place up." She squatted down and scratched Gus's ears. "Think I could have that back?"

It looked doubtful.

She turned to me. "Can he have a snack? Maybe he'd trade the sweater for a cookie."

"I'm pretty sure he'd trade me for a cookie," I told her.

She laughed. She rummaged around in her desk and pulled out a package of animal crackers.

Gus's ears perked up when she opened the package. He spit that sweater out like it tasted nasty when she offered him a cookie.

I snatched the sweater. "It has some drool on it."

She gave Gus a second cookie. "It'll wash." She gave him one more. "Thank you so much for your help. The next time I lose something, you'll be the first person I call."

I felt a foot taller.

"The rain's stopped," she told me. "Just a passing shower. Better get him outside before I get in trouble."

I didn't want that. She was very nice.

"I'll just take these up front and meet you at the desk." She scooped up my books and checked the hallway to make sure it was empty. She motioned us out.

Gus and I went outside, and I tied him back to the bench,

which was sitting a little crooked. "No more shenanigans," I warned him.

His tongue lolled out of his mouth. I was pretty sure that meant *No promises*.

"I just need to see your library card," Ms. Caroline said once I'd made it back to the counter.

Oops. How had I forgotten that? "I'd like to get a library card, please," I told her.

"Okay. What's your home address?"

The question pierced me like an arrow. Did I even have a home anymore? Someone else was living in our apartment. I'd never stayed with Dad more than a few days in a row. I had no idea how long Nana Pat and Papaw Jack were going to let me stay with them.

Maybe I didn't belong anywhere.

"Glory?"

I blinked. My face was hot and my palms were sweaty and my heart galloped around my rib cage like it didn't know where it belonged either.

"Um, I'm staying with my grandparents. Pat and Jack Ewing?" I couldn't remember their address.

Ms. Caroline lit up. "You're Pat and Jack's granddaughter? Well, I should have known. You look a lot like your mama did when she was your age."

"You knew my mom?" Sometimes I forgot my mom had lived an entire life here before she'd moved to Baton Rouge.

"I sure did. My daughter went to school with her. What is she up to these days?"

My mouth went dry. "She's on vacation." Was it really a

lie if I was just repeating what everyone had told me? Even if I didn't believe it?

"Good for her." She smiled at me. "Come back with your grandma and we can get you a card."

My shoulders slumped. I didn't want to leave without these books.

"I'll check them out for you."

I turned around. The girl from the park was standing behind me.

"Rosemary!"

She seemed happy that I remembered her name.

"What are you doing here?" I asked.

She pointed to the window. Lydie and Sebastian were sitting on the bench keeping Gus company. I hoped he didn't decide to drag them all over town. "Story time." She took her library card out of her pocket.

"Oh, no, that's okay," I told her.

"I don't mind. I owe you one anyway. For helping Sebastian the other day."

That was all Gus.

"Are you sure?" Ms. Caroline asked her. "You'll be responsible for the books."

Rosemary grinned. "I don't think she looks like a book thief." She eyed me suspiciously. "Are you the kind of person who dog-ears pages?" She had a little mischievous glint in her eyes.

"Never," I said solemnly. "I use a bookmark like a responsible person." I tried to look extra responsible as I smiled at Ms. Caroline.

Rosemary slid the books over in front of her. "I'd like to check these out, please."

"Thank you," I whispered. I wasn't used to people I'd just met doing me favors. Ms. Caroline bent the rules to give Gus and me a place to stay dry. Rosemary was trusting me not to lose these books. Sweet Olive was turning out to be a not-so-bad place.

Rosemary looked pleased.

"They're due in three weeks," Ms. Caroline said. She looked each one of us in the eye.

"I will return them in two," I promised. I was going to learn everything I could about tracking by then.

Rosemary followed me outside. "Y'all are very good babysitters," I told Lydie and Sebastian.

"I'm good at most things," Lydie said.

I liked that kind of confidence. Rosemary rolled her eyes, but I could tell she was trying not to laugh.

"Better hurry if you want the good spot on the carpet," Rosemary told them.

Sebastian whispered something in Gus's ear, and Gus looked so serious, like it was a secret he appreciated being told. "Can Gus come play sometime?" he asked me.

"Gus would like that very much."

Sebastian's smile was bigger than he was. I gave Rosemary my number so we could set it up later.

"You are very popular," I told Gus as we walked home. It was impossible to feel lonely with him around.

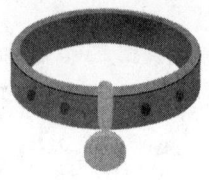

CHAPTER SEVEN

I stayed up late that night reading all about training bloodhounds to track. It was a lot more work than I'd imagined. I showed Gus pictures from the books and talked to him about what it said we were supposed to do.

"Bloodhounds used to be called St. Hubert hounds," I told Gus. "Like me: St. Romain!" That just proved Gus and I were meant to find each other. "Have you ever found a real missing person before?"

He cocked his head.

"This says you are an expert at finding missing people." I wished more than anything that meant he could help me find Mom. But she hadn't just recently wandered off. It was going to take more than a powerful nose to track her down.

And then what? Even if I did figure out where she went, I couldn't make her come home.

I couldn't make her want to stay with me.

Gus lifted his paw and patted my knee lightly.

"Yes?"

He patted me again.

I set the book down. "Oh. Do you want pets?"

He blinked at me, like maybe he thought I wasn't as smart as he was. I reached over and rubbed his chest. He had a huge, deep chest that stuck out.

"Okay, let's get started, you and I." I stopped petting him and grabbed my notebook. I flipped it open to what I knew. It wasn't much. I wrote *Last place I saw Mom*, then drew a line under it. I wrote down *At home, before I went to school, May 6.*

Gus was a bit more forceful with his paw this time.

"You sure are demanding," I said, petting him some more. I sighed. "I'm sorry I said that. You're probably just missing Mr. Babin. I wish you could understand me more than you already do. Then you'd know that he didn't want to leave you."

That was a harder thing to understand—why people left if they had a choice to stay.

I settled against the foot of the bed and rubbed Gus with my left hand while writing in my notebook with my right. "Since we don't know where she is, let's start with what we know for sure—where she isn't."

She wasn't at Nana Pat and Papaw Jack's. She hadn't been here in over a year. Maybe Nana Pat wasn't telling me everything she knew, but I didn't think she was lying about that.

She wasn't at home. Someone else was living in our apartment now. She wasn't at Jimmy's Grill.

That left a whole wide world where she could be.

I had no idea where to even start. But she knew how to find me. I had the same phone number I'd had since my tenth birthday, when Dad gave me a phone. Why hadn't she called?

Did Mom miss me at all?

I shut my notebook. Fictional detectives made this look a lot easier than it was turning out to be.

I wondered where Dad was right then. His postcard had arrived, from a place called Bug Tussle, Texas. I'd tacked it up on the bulletin board with the rest of them. But Dad wasn't in Bug Tussle. He would be several states away by now.

The world was very big, and my parents were very far away. If I thought too hard about all that space between us, I felt very small.

It was late, but I didn't want to get in bed. I grabbed my pillow and blanket and snuggled up next to Gus on the floor. I finally fell asleep, soothed by the lullaby of Gus's snores.

Gus and I tromped down the stairs the next morning ready for a proper training session. I'd decided to work with him in the backyard to avoid distractions. Eventually distractions would be good, but right now, Gus needed to understand what I wanted him to do before he could do it with cross scents and noise.

We both had a lot to learn.

Papaw Jack didn't look up as we passed the den. The blinds were shut tight and the lights were off, the only glow coming from the television.

The doldrums, Nana Pat called them, when Papaw Jack

went into his cocoon and hid from people. She said they'd come up more and more since his stroke. Papaw Jack was having trouble adjusting to this new way.

The kitchen was empty. Nana Pat liked to go for walks in the morning—to get her blood pumping early, she'd always say—so I brought Gus's food bowl in and set it next to the table. I didn't want to eat breakfast alone.

I poured myself a bowl of cereal, and Gus and I munched our way through breakfast side by side. He finished his much faster than I did, of course. I'd given him slightly less than usual too, since he would be getting plenty of treats during training. I rinsed my cereal bowl while Gus drank water, then I let him into the backyard to run around and do his business.

I sat on a patio chair and watched Gus wander. He liked to sniff every inch of the fence that ringed the backyard. I called it doing his morning patrol. When he was done making sure no intruders had invaded his space, he sat facing whatever breeze was blowing and enjoyed the day.

His face was so sweet and regal. Sometimes he lifted his chin and let the breeze blow his ears. Sometimes he looked up and watched a bird soar overhead. Most of the time he peered through the fence and kept an eye on the neighbors.

I joined Gus in the grass. He glanced at me as I folded myself to the ground, but then he went back to his observations. Gus was curious about the world, like I was. I wished I knew what he was thinking.

Nana Pat's flowers shone bright in the sun, and her vegetable garden, which was out beside the shed, was starting to get thick and full. Papaw Jack used to be in charge of the garden, but Nana Pat took over after his stroke. When she got back from her walk, she'd wade into the rows and pull weeds and check on the plants' progress. I wanted to get in a couple of runs before she came back.

But I had to make flags first.

The book said I needed tracking flags to show where the trail was so that I could make sure Gus was doing it right. I didn't have any tracking flags, but I could improvise. I went into the kitchen and took several forks out of the drawer. I'd found a box of yarn in the closet in my room. I sat on the bench in the backyard and cut pieces of purple yarn. I tied them to the handle of the forks.

We would definitely have to be done before Nana Pat got home.

"Gus, come," I said.

Gus looked at me and went back to doing exactly what he wanted to.

I sighed. Bloodhounds were hardheaded.

"Treat?"

Gus decided he wanted to come see me after all.

I'd cut up a couple of hot dogs for treats, and I lured him into the laundry room with one. I shut him in. Gus howled in protest.

"It's just for a minute," I told him. He needed to stay inside while I laid the trail; otherwise he would just follow behind me and eat the treats as soon as I dropped them.

It wasn't easy getting the forks in the ground, but after a couple of tries I managed to plant a fork at the start of the trail. The bright purple I'd tied at the top fluttered in the breeze. I shuffled my feet and dropped a treat and another flag. I did this several more times, keeping the trail fairly straight. When I got to the end, I dropped one of my socks and put a scoop of dog food on top of it. Then I followed the flags back to the start so that I wasn't laying random trails on my way back.

I did it exactly the way the book said.

I slipped inside the laundry room. Gus tried to get out the door past me, but I grabbed his collar. "Don't bolt," I told him. "Just let me get your leash on."

The book said we needed a harness and a really long leash, but we had to make do with what we had.

I opened the back door and held on to Gus's collar so he couldn't get ahead of me. I took him to the start of the trail, then stuck another sock in front of his face. "Find it," I told Gus. "Find it." I repeated it so he could learn the command.

He immediately put his head down and went to sniffing. He found the flags—one, two, three—and went straight to the sock, no detours.

"Good boy!" I said, elated. I rubbed his head. "You're so smart!"

The trail had been very short and Gus had probably just followed the smell of hot dogs rather than me, but it was a solid start.

When we walked back toward the house, I saw that Papaw Jack's blinds were up.

I left Gus in the backyard as I laid another trail just outside the fence. When I looked over, Gus was peering through one of the slats. "I'm pretty sure that's cheating," I told him. He didn't look the least bit ashamed.

I led him through the side gate. I gave him the sock to sniff. "Find it." He sniffed to the first flag and gobbled the hot dog. He took his time looking for more pieces of hot dog before heading to the second. But before we got to the third flag, Edna Gill's cat slunk around the side of the house.

Gus froze, nose twitching. "Don't even think about it," I growled.

He was more than thinking about it. With a loud bay, he tore off after the cat. "Gus, no!" I shouted, holding tight to the leash and running after him. The cat darted away, and Gus got to the end of the leash. He didn't stop.

I held on, but now that all the slack had run out, Gus dragged me down. I was pretty sure he would have dragged me halfway across Sweet Olive, but the cat managed to make it up a tree, and Gus stood at the bottom of it, baying.

I got to my feet and dusted myself off. Both knees were covered in dirt, but neither was bleeding. I grabbed Gus's collar. "Bad dog," I said, though I couldn't be sure he could even hear me over all the racket he was making. "You do not chase cats."

Gus looked back at me, his expression clearly saying that yes, he did chase cats, wasn't I just witness to that very fact?

I pulled him away from the tree. It wasn't easy. He was bigger than I was, and I was pretty sure he knew it. "You do not get the rest of the treats," I told him. I managed to get him back into the backyard. I locked the gate behind him before picking up the flags and uneaten treats.

Papaw Jack was in the backyard with Gus when I came back through the gate.

"Good morning!" I said.

He grunted. "Racket."

"Yeah, sorry about that."

"Escaped con?" Papaw Jack's mouth twitched a little. Maybe that meant he was feeling better.

I rolled my eyes. "Not quite. A cat."

Papaw Jack scratched Gus behind the ears. "Darn cat," he said, seeming to sympathize with Gus. "She eats my birds."

Papaw Jack had a bird feeder hanging just outside his den window, though with the shades drawn most of the time, I didn't figure he got in much bird-watching.

Papaw Jack shuffled to the garden bench and sat down. He'd brought a thermos outside, and he poured himself a cup of coffee. He offered it to me.

"No thanks. I tasted coffee once, but it's like drinking hot water poured through dirty gym socks."

Papaw Jack took a sip and sighed, closing his eyes and turning his face up to the sun. "Good gym socks."

I laughed. Papaw Jack was kind of funny, in his own way.

"What are you doing?" he asked, eyeing the forks I was holding.

I put them in my lap with an apologetic smile. I explained about tracking. I told him why I needed the forks. "I think Mr. Babin will be really happy if I can train Gus to find people."

I didn't say anything about how badly I wished Gus were mine for real and forever. I did not tell him why the idea of finding lost people mattered to me.

Sometimes the things we didn't say were the most true of all.

While Papaw Jack and I talked, Gus stalked the fence. I was pretty sure he was hoping that cat would drop down within reach.

"He's big," Papaw Jack said, watching Gus trample a little on Nana Pat's squash plants. "You're not."

"That's why I'm dirty," I told him. "He pulled me down. But we're working on it. If I can train him well enough, he'll mostly listen and not pull me down."

"Mostly?"

"Well, all the books say that bloodhounds have to be stubborn and not listen if they're going to stay on the trail. They have to trust their own noses. And we have to trust our dogs."

Papaw nodded his head, like I'd said something profound rather than something I'd just picked up from a library book.

Gus was easy to trust. The adults in my life? Not so much. I knew they thought they were doing the right thing, but Dad knew more than he was telling me. Maybe Nana Pat and Papaw Jack did too.

And the fact was, none of them had been a steady presence in my life. So I could only trust what I knew. And what I knew was that people left.

"Want to play hide-and-seek?" Papaw Jack asked all of a sudden.

"What?"

"I'll hide." He pointed to Gus. "He'll seek."

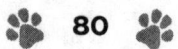

"I don't know if he's ready for that."

Papaw Jack shrugged his left shoulder. "Just practice."

"Okay." I explained to him about laying a trail. "And shuffle your feet to leave a lot of scent. He's not very good yet."

"They only shuffle these days," he said, but there was humor in his face.

"And drop your hat at the start so he'll have something to follow." I grabbed Gus by the collar and steered him back inside. I didn't want either one of us to see where Papaw Jack was hiding.

I waited with Gus just inside the door. "You're going to find Papaw Jack," I said, stroking his head. He closed his eyes and leaned into my hand, so I rubbed his ear. He sighed, eyes still closed. Something in my heart squeezed a little bit. I leaned down and kissed the tip of his nose.

I waited another minute past the time I thought Papaw should be hidden, then peeked out the window to make sure he was gone. His hat was abandoned on the ground.

"Okay, Gus. Showtime." I held tight to his collar and led him to the hat. He was already sniffing it before I picked it up. I held that hat in front of his nose. "Find it, Gus. Find it."

He looked up at me. I showed him the hat again. "Find Papaw Jack."

Gus's head went down and I could hear him snorting and sniffing. He veered one way, then another, and because I hadn't been looking, I had no idea if he was staying on the trail or not.

He pulled me to the first trail I'd laid and rooted around in the grass. I was pretty sure he was hoping to find more pieces of hot dog. I tugged him away. "Find Papaw Jack."

He started toward the shed, head down, and for a minute I thought he was going to bonk his head into the shed door. But then he veered off to the right, tugging me into the small space between the fence and the shed.

He got distracted by some weeds. I tried not to get frustrated.

Papaw Jack cleared his throat. Gus took off, tail wagging madly as he rounded the corner of the shed.

When I'd caught up, I found Papaw Jack scratching Gus's scruff. He reached into his pocket and gave Gus a treat. Both of them seemed pretty proud of themselves.

"Good boy, Gus!" I said, my voice rising in excitement even though Papaw Jack cheated a little. "You found him!" I patted Gus's side and gave him a couple more treats. I wanted him to know he'd get rewarded for doing a good job. If nothing else, this dog was motivated by food.

"I think that's enough for today," I told Gus. Two out of three finds was pretty good, for our first try. "Let's get some water." Gus followed me toward the house. I turned back to Papaw Jack. "You coming?"

He was bending over in the garden. He stood up with a couple of weeds in his hand, which he tossed over the back fence. "In a bit."

CHAPTER EIGHT

Nana Pat didn't work weekends unless it was an emergency, so that meant on weekends she was a tornado of activity. I mostly tried to stay out of her way, since if I hovered too long anywhere else, Nana Pat tried to recruit me into her cleaning schemes. She'd already cleaned out the fridge this morning and was now trying to wipe the finish off the kitchen counters.

Maybe she worried she would simply wind down to nothing if she sat still for longer than ten minutes. She eyed the vacuum cleaner she'd pulled out of the closet. Looked at Gus. I knew what she was thinking. She's taken to vacuuming every single day because, as she said, "That dogs sheds more than any creature on this planet. How is he not bald by now?"

Maybe Gus suspected that he was about to be vacuumed, because he peeled himself off the kitchen floor where he'd been snoozing (and trying to break Nana Pat's neck, according to Nana Pat) and barreled into Papaw Jack's den.

I hurried after him. I didn't want him to bother Papaw Jack. Gus and I had to make sure not to aggravate anyone. I didn't want Gus sent away. And I didn't have anywhere else to go either. What would I do if Nana Pat and Papaw Jack decided Gus and I were too much trouble?

"Sorry, Papaw Jack," I said. "I'll get him out."

"Stay," he said.

I let Gus explore and folded to the floor on the left side of Papaw Jack's chair. He saw better out of his left eye. He could see mostly fine out of his right eye if he was looking straight ahead—it was when he tried to look sideways that he had trouble.

I wondered if Nana Pat had gained what he'd lost. Because she had no problem with the side-eye whatsoever.

Papaw Jack nodded at me, and the left side of his mouth moved into what I now knew was a smile.

"Anything good on?" The TV cast flickering shadows across the dimly lit room.

Papaw made a face and shook his head. Gus sidled over and plopped down with his back to Papaw Jack. When Papaw Jack didn't immediately start petting Gus, Gus leaned his head back and looked at him.

"He wants pets," I told Papaw Jack.

He reached out with his left hand and scratched the top of Gus's head, then ran his hand along his back. I looked around the room. Papaw Jack's den was lined with bookshelves. I could see history books and horror books and lots of science fiction.

Papaw Jack had to have been lonely sitting in this den by himself every day. He and Nana Pat were hard workers, and after Papaw Jack retired from the plant, he'd stayed busy working in his garden or out in his shop. But all that stopped when he'd had his stroke. Nana Pat couldn't sit still for long, bustling off to do laundry or clean the kitchen or cook something.

That left Papaw Jack alone in here.

His gnarled and weathered hand rested on Gus's side as Gus leaned against his knee.

It was almost impossible to be lonely with Gus in the room. He took up space—and never once felt bad about that. He sniffed and drooled and scooched into places. He made sure everyone knew he was there. He never tried to make himself smaller for someone else.

And even if his first family hadn't appreciated that, I did.

I spotted a row of familiar titles and jumped to my feet for a closer look. "You like Agatha Christie?"

"Yep," he said.

"Me too!" The only other person I knew who liked Agatha Christie was the school librarian who'd loaned me her books. "Which one is your favorite?"

He was silent for a while. Gus flopped over on his side and went to sleep. I didn't know if Papaw Jack was trying to decide his favorite or trying to remember its title or just looking for the word.

"*Orient Express*," he finally said.

"I just finished that one! It was great! But I like *Death on the Nile* better." I wandered down the row and looked at his books. "Have you ever read Gale Fox?"

"I don't think so."

"She writes really great mysteries. The main character is

a thirteen-year-old detective. I've read all of them at least three times. I only have the first one, but you can borrow it if you want."

"Thank you. But maybe the library. I need big print now."

I looked at the rows and rows of books. It made me sad to think he couldn't read most of them anymore. Books were very good company.

The built-in bookshelves sat on top of a single row of cabinets. I opened and shut a few.

Papaw Jack didn't call me nosy like Nana Pat might have. But I was looking for clues to a lot of different mysteries—who Nana Pat and Papaw Jack were, where my mom was, where I belonged—and the only way to learn those things was to look and listen.

Nana Pat and Papaw Jack had a lot of stuff. They would have, living in the same house for so long. I found blankets and stacks of old magazines and even an old DVD player.

And a small stack of puzzles.

"Do you like puzzles?" I asked.

He turned to see what I was looking at.

"Never done one."

"Really? You should. It sounds boring but it's actually pretty fun." I riffled through the boxes. A pretty woods scene, the beach, and one with a dog sitting in front of a cabin in the mountains. "Whose are these, then?"

"Probably your mom's."

It shouldn't have felt strange to find so much of Mom's stuff in the house where she'd grown up. But it did.

"Want to try one?"

At first, I thought Papaw Jack was going to say no. Instead, he turned off the TV and got to his feet. He switched on another light. I took the puzzle to the table at the back of the den. It was a smaller kitchen table, but the perfect size for this puzzle. Gus, not wanting to be left out, followed us and crawled underneath the table, his head toward my feet and his tail lying along the tops of Papaw Jack's slippers.

I dumped the puzzle out onto the table and flipped the lid over so we could see what we were working toward.

"First we do the frame," I told him, "since those with flat sides are easy to find. Then we can organize by color. It's easier that way."

He followed my lead, separating the edges from the rest. At first, he was using only his left hand, but then he began to use his right too. It didn't really matter that his right one didn't work as well. He wasn't gripping or holding anything, just using it to slide puzzle pieces this way and that. It wasn't long before we were in a rhythm.

"Mom and I used to do puzzles together," I told him. "Though not always at the same time. She worked a lot and weird hours sometimes, so I'd work on it when I got home from school and she'd work on it after I'd gone to bed." Sometimes I'd wake up in the morning and rush out to see how much she'd gotten done, feeling a little like I did when I woke up on my birthday or Christmas. "She'd always let me put in the last piece."

But I'd done my last couple of puzzles entirely by myself. I'd waited days to see if she'd added a piece. She never did.

Nana Pat fired up the vacuum and tangoed past the den. Papaw Jack and I worked in silence for a while.

"Why didn't we come for Christmas last year?" I finally asked.

Papaw Jack slid two edge pieces out of the jumble and put them off to the side. "You'd have to ask your mom."

I had. She'd ignored me. And now she wasn't here, and I had so many questions for her that I wouldn't even know which one to start with.

Actually, that wasn't true. The first thing I'd ask Mom if she ever answered her phone would be the only one that mattered right now—*where are you?*

Papaw Jack cleared his throat. "I named you."

That was not what I'd expected him to say. He smiled his lopsided smile. He was doing more of that these days. Probably because of Gus. He made us all smile more. Even Nana Pat.

Papaw Jack spoke slowly and carefully, and because I wanted to hear this story, I was very patient. "I was there the day you were born. Your mom was so young." His smile dimmed a little, like the sun being briefly covered by a cloud. I remembered I wasn't the only one Mom had left. "She handed you to me. You were the tiniest thing. I stood at the window and watched the sun rise. It was glorious. I told you to look at the sunrise. And you did!" He laughed. "You opened your eyes. And smiled! Only a few hours old. So you became Gloria Dawn."

It was the most I'd heard Papaw Jack say since I'd arrived. He must have thought these words were very important.

For me, that story meant I'd had a family at the very beginning.

"So what happened?" I asked. He was there when I was born. Mom had trusted him to name me. We used to come visit. And then I didn't see him for a long time.

Papaw Jack sighed, deep and long and bleak. "The adults messed up."

I wasn't sure what that meant.

"Nana Pat likes bossing and your mom doesn't like being told what to do."

I could see how that could have been a problem. "They're stubborn," I said.

"Exactly." He shook his head. "And I guess I'm not stubborn enough. I should have fought harder." His eyes slid to his right arm, which was lying in his lap. That look said he thought his stroke stole all his fight. But I didn't think that was true. All these pieces I was seeing, all these clues I was learning, told a different story. I thought Papaw Jack had more fight in him than most.

I thought maybe he had just lost track of it for a while.

"Fought harder for what?" I asked.

"For you."

Gus and I went upstairs after lunch. I took out my notebook of clues and added where my name had come from. I couldn't see how it fit into this puzzle, but that was how clues worked. It took more than one to show the whole picture.

I'd listened to the rest of what Papaw Jack had said—and what he hadn't. It sounded like Nana Pat and Mom had had a fight, which meant that not seeing them for a year had more to do with Mom than me.

That shouldn't have made me feel better, but it did.

Papaw Jack thought I was worth fighting for.

Gus sighed.

"Are you bored?" I closed my notebook and put it back under the bed. Gus didn't lift his head, just sighed again. I took the tracking book off my nightstand and read to him for a little while. He didn't even wag his tail once.

"I think Gus is sad," I said as I came into the kitchen, Gus trailing behind me. Nana Pat and Papaw Jack were both sitting at the table with cups of coffee. Maybe that was the secret to Nana Pat's constant energy. We all looked at Gus, who blinked morosely at us.

"I think that's just his face," said Nana Pat. "He's got more wrinkles than sense."

"I want to take him to the hospital to see Mr. Babin."

Nana Pat looked horrified. "I will not be sneaking a dog into the hospital."

"Not inside." I adored Gus, but I did not trust him inside a hospital. His personality was just too big for that. "We could stand outside the window, show Mr. Babin I'm taking good care of him."

Nana Pat still looked doubtful.

"I think it would make Gus feel better."

"Well, if it'll make Gus happy, then by all means. He has a tough life, sleeping inside most of the day, eating treats you sneak him from the dinner table." She raised an eyebrow at my expression. "I've been around a long time. I see things."

"Please?"

"I'm not putting him in my car."

"We can take my truck," said Papaw Jack.

And that settled it.

"We're going for a ride!" I told Gus. He jumped to his feet, and I snapped his leash on him. I was pretty sure he knew what a ride was. He pulled and tugged the leash, then marched us right to Papaw Jack's truck. I opened the back door, and Gus put his front paws on the floorboard.

"He can ride in the bed of the truck," Nana Pat said.

"It's not safe!" I argued. "Please let him ride in the back seat with me."

In the end, it was Papaw Jack who convinced her, not me. I was learning that Papaw Jack didn't ask for much, but when he did, he mostly got it. Maybe that was because he only asked for things that really mattered.

"Jump up," I told Gus. He stomped one of his hind legs, then looked over his shoulder at me. "You have got to be kidding me." I laughed, then hoisted Gus's backside into the truck.

Gus climbed right up on the seat, and I slid in beside him. Nana Pat cranked the truck. Papaw Jack couldn't drive anymore because of his stroke. Soon we were cruising through the neighborhood, Gus drooling on the window.

Papaw Jack glanced back at us and grinned, like this was one of the best adventures he'd been on in a while.

I leaned over and rolled Gus's window down a little. He

stuck his head out. His ears flapped in the breeze. Nana Pat looked at him in her side mirror, and I saw her grin.

She looked much younger when she smiled like that.

Gus started to sing. He closed his eyes, head still out the window, ears still flying behind him like flags, and sang his heart out.

My heart sang out as well, joy bubbling up inside me as I watched Gus. My joy wasn't nearly as loud as his was, but it was there.

Funny how joy could sneak up on a person like that. Worry filled up a lot of space inside me these days, but joy made sure I knew it was still there.

Nana Pat and Papaw Jack were both laughing. Because joy wasn't only sneaky—it was contagious.

"They're going to think we're an ambulance when we pull in," Nana Pat said.

The hospital was just outside town, between Sweet Olive and Mead. It wasn't very big, nothing like the hospitals in Baton Rouge.

"Mr. Babin is in room 124," Nana Pat told me as she parked the truck. "That's on the other side of the building. I'll go in and let him know. The windows don't open, so you'll just have to wave at him from outside."

I climbed out of the back seat first, then held tight to Gus's leash as he sort of jump-fell out of the back. It wasn't that long of a walk to the other side of the building, but Gus took his sweet time, sniffing and searching, which meant Papaw Jack could keep up with us just fine.

Windows lined the other side of the building, and I

couldn't be sure which one belonged to Mr. Babin. Gus and I waited.

Nana Pat waved at one of the windows, and I walked Gus forward. Nana Pat stepped back, and I could see Mr. Babin sitting up in his bed. He was wearing a blue robe, and his white hair was sticking up. His face lit up when he saw Gus. He waved.

"Look, Gus," I said as I led him even closer to the window. "It's Mr. Babin."

I tapped the window, and Gus looked up. I could tell the moment he saw Mr. Babin. His tail wagged harder and harder.

I couldn't help but grin. "Say hi," I told him.

Gus pulled me closer to the window, then reared up and put his paws on the windowsill.

Mr. Babin was smiling and waving and saying something. We couldn't hear his words, but that didn't matter. We knew what he meant. He was happy too.

Gus bayed, a cross between a bark and a howl, loud and raucous. It sounded like joy.

Mr. Babin laughed.

We stayed that way for fifteen minutes or so, just saying hi through the window, until Gus got bored and pulled me away after a smell. "Bye!" I shouted, hoping Mr. Babin understood.

"Look over there," Papaw Jack said.

I turned to where he was pointing. An old woman was waving at Gus from her window. Papaw Jack and I waved back. Gus was wagging his tail, so I thought that counted as a wave.

The curtains were closed on the next two windows, but a little girl was peering out of the last one. She looked tiny in the big hospital bed, but there was nothing small about her smile when she saw Gus. She was missing her two front teeth.

I pulled Gus to a stop and waved. The girl waved back. The lady sitting by the girl's bed, who was probably her mom, turned, and her face lifted in surprise. She was holding the little girl's hand.

My next breath hurt as if it had ragged edges. I pretended it didn't.

"Look, Gus." He lifted his head, and the little girl blew him a kiss.

I was pretty sure dogs were put on this planet to help us through the tough times.

"I think this was a very good idea," I told Papaw Jack as Gus tugged me back toward the truck. For Mr. Babin and Gus and everyone else who'd needed a drooling, wrinkled, furry ball of chaos to brighten their day.

"The best," he agreed.

Nana Pat was waiting for us by the truck.

"Ready to go home?" I asked Gus.

It took me a second to realize what I'd said. But it really was starting to feel like somewhere I belonged. Here, with Gus.

I only wondered what that meant when summer was over.

CHAPTER NINE

I kept a box under the bed of all the stuff I'd taken when I had to leave our apartment. I hadn't even opened it since the day I'd packed it. It was mostly junk anyway, everything I'd grabbed in a panic when I realized I wouldn't be coming back to our apartment. Ever.

I slid it out from under the bed. It was a fairly small box to contain the last little bits of my old life. Now I was going to comb through all the unimportant stuff Mom had left behind to see if maybe there were clues.

I pulled the tape off the box and began digging through it. Magnets off the fridge. A take-out menu. (No idea why I'd thought I'd need that.) The stack of mail that had been by the coffeepot.

They were mostly late bills, a bright red stamp across the front of several. I opened a credit card bill. The card was maxed out. I ran my finger along the charges. Mom had been paying the rent with the card. And when she ran out of credit, she couldn't pay the rent.

That was why we'd gotten evicted.

My stomach hurt. The next notice was from the bank. *Overdrawn* was typed in bold. Mom had -$127.32 in her account. The date at the top was from three days before she'd left.

Some detective I was. I'd always thought I was observant, but I'd missed everything. She'd gotten fired and run out of money. All these late bills just showed she hadn't found a new job. All those times I thought she was just tired from work—she was probably worried because she couldn't find work and pay her bills.

Thinking back, I could see all the clues I'd missed at the time. She was sad. Stressed. There was less food in the house. She lost her temper more.

Once, I'd heard her crying after I'd gone to bed.

Why hadn't she asked Dad for help? Or Nana Pat and Papaw Jack?

Why had she run away from everything and left me alone rather than simply ask for a little bit of help? I was furious at her for not answering her phone, for not saying goodbye, for not telling me what was going on. I was old enough to understand.

She'd been trying her best—I could see that. But when her very best wasn't enough, rather than trust someone else, she'd just walked away, leaving me here with all of the mess and none of the answers.

It wasn't fair.

I pushed the box away from me. I didn't know if I was angrier at Mom for leaving or at myself for not seeing what was going on and trying to help her. More than anything, I wished I'd been enough to make her stay.

Gus stuck his head in the box. "Hi," I said. He wagged his tail and shoved the bills around with his nose. Gus probably would have sensed exactly what had been going on. He pulled his head out of the box and stuck his nose in my face. He sniffed my face, maybe checking to see I hadn't eaten a snack without sharing, then gave me a very wet kiss. Gross, but it did make me feel a little bit better.

Even if Mom didn't want me around, Gus did.

He shifted so I could rub his head, his tail beating hard against the wall. "You're going to damage either yourself or that wall," I told him, but really, how could I even think about fussing at his happiness?

That was one of the things I loved about Gus. He didn't really let much bother him. He existed fully in this world, loved and made messes and sniffed every single scent the world had to offer. He didn't apologize if he was too loud or took up too much space.

We could learn a lot from dogs.

He moved forward, tail still wagging, beating out a rhythm on the wall.

Only now it was a different sound.

And I had read enough detective novels to know what that meant.

"That one's loose," I told him. My heart was beating harder. Was this how all detectives felt when they were hot on a case? The walls were wooden planks on the top half but wooden panels on the bottom. I rapped on the first panel. It made a solid noise. I rapped on the second panel, and it had more of an empty sound. Like it might be hollow. The panel itself rattled faintly.

I stuck my fingers into the narrow slot on the side and wiggled and pulled and wiggled and pulled. It moved. Gus stuck his big head close to the wall.

"Not helping, Gus," I grunted as I kept pulling.

It fell free.

The wall inside was dusty and unfinished. Pink insulation hung down. And in the very bottom there was a large book.

"Gus, you really are the best detective ever," I told him, rubbing his ears. I reached in to pull out the book.

Top Secret was written across the front in marker. I opened it.

The first page had *Layla's Dream Book* written in bubble letters. And underneath it was a picture of the Eiffel Tower.

I flipped the page. My mom had made this, maybe when she was my age. She'd cut out pictures from magazines and books of all the cool places she'd wanted to go. There were pictures of marine biologists and a brochure for some college in North Carolina.

She'd doodled pictures and written out goals and listed her wishes. There were so many.

I realized what I was looking at. It was all the things my mom had wanted to do when she grew up.

I only had to turn to the third page to realize she hadn't done a single one of them.

She'd had such big plans—and they'd fallen apart. Looking

at all these beautiful places that existed in this world, seeing the hope sprinkled across these pages, glimpsing confidence in Mom's bold handwriting—I realized maybe she hadn't given up.

Maybe she'd just decided to start over.

I took a very big breath. What if she hadn't left me for good? What if, once she was settled in one of these new places, she was coming to get me?

The tiniest spark of hope kindled to life. I imagined my mom in a brand-new place, with a job and an apartment that didn't smell musty. With furniture that hadn't been someone else's first, then someone else's second, before it was ours.

Maybe she hadn't told me anything because she wanted it to be a surprise. She'd gotten knocked down, but what if she was getting back on her feet somewhere? And when she did, she'd show up for me.

If Mom wasn't giving up on her dreams, then I wasn't going to give up on Mom.

I grabbed my phone, part of me expecting a text or missed call. But there was nothing.

She must have needed more time.

Maybe Mom still wanted me after all.

"Glory!" Nana Pat called up the stairs sometime later. "Come down here a minute."

I covered the late bills with Mom's dream book and

shoved it all under the bed. I didn't want to put the book back in the wall.

Gus, who'd been sleeping like it was his full-time job, grunted and stretched. "I'll bring us up a snack," I promised.

He opened one eye, watched me for a moment, then let it fall closed again.

Nana Pat was in the kitchen with a woman I didn't know. The woman smiled when I came in. "You've gotten so big!"

I smiled politely. I didn't know who she was, but considering I hadn't been to visit in a while, of course I'd gotten bigger. That was what kids did—we grew.

"Glory, do you remember your aunt Kat?"

I blinked. "I have an aunt?"

"A great-aunt," Nana Pat said.

The woman winked at me. "The greatest."

Nana Pat rolled her eyes, but she was smiling. And there was something in that smile that made me see the resemblance between her and Aunt Kat, though mostly they looked like night and day. Nana Pat was angular and wore her face like a uniform; Aunt Kat was round and soft and looked halfway to another joke already.

"Aunt Kat is my younger sister."

It was strange, imagining Nana Pat with other family. With a sister.

"You were missing most of your teeth the last time I saw you," Aunt Kat said. "When was that, Patty?"

"Patty?" I said.

Aunt Kat looked at Nana Pat in surprise—and something like trouble twinkled in her eye. I decided I liked Aunt Kat.

"Didn't you know?" she asked me. "Her nickname growing up was Patty Cakes."

I cackled before I could stop myself. If I had spent a month of Sundays alone in my room trying to come up with nicknames for Nana Pat, I still never would have come up with Patty Cakes. She didn't look like a Patty or a Cake. I decided I would need way more time to have Nana Pat all figured out.

"No one has called me that since I was ten."

"I call you that all the time."

"No one who counts."

Aunt Kat pouted. "I count more than most people."

"Tell her your nickname, then."

Aunt Kat waved her hand in the air. "Oh, I have way too many to know which one you mean. And half of them aren't meant for young ears." She leaned over and whispered loud enough for me to hear. "They're all just jealous."

"They called us Patty and Katty most of the time."

"Well, I'm only a little catty," Aunt Kat said.

Gus trotted into the kitchen. Aunt Kat looked at Gus as if he were a rare and nearly extinct creature who'd just wandered into Buckingham Palace.

"You finally woke up?" I asked.

He gave a very large yawn. Gus was a smidge dramatic.

Aunt Kat glanced at Nana Pat, obviously looking for an answer. Nana Pat threw up her hands. "This is Gus. Glory is dog-sitting him for a while."

Aunt Kat laughed. "And he stays in the house?"

I nodded, and Nana Pat sighed. Aunt Kat laughed again.

Her entire body shook as she threw back her head and let her laugh just roll out of her. I didn't think I had ever seen anyone so pleased about something, in that full-bellied way of laughing that made everyone around them happier too. She wiped at her eyes and stood up. "I never thought I'd see the day," Aunt Kat said, and she pulled me into a hug. She was tall and soft and strong, and it might have been one of the best hugs of my life. "A little dog hair just might be good for you," she said over my head.

"It's more than a little," Nana Pat assured her.

Gus did shed a lot more than I knew dogs could. I'd been expecting to find bald spots on him at any moment, considering the amount of hair I found on my clothes and the floor and his bed. But I guessed he kept regrowing it overnight.

"Oooh, I'll have to bring over Mervin," Aunt Kat said, sitting back down. Gus planted his drooly head in her lap, and rather than grossed out, she looked thrilled.

"Absolutely not." Nana Pat's voice was stern.

"Who's Mervin?" I asked.

"My dog." Aunt Kat was rubbing Gus's ears and he was making happy noises.

"You have a dog?"

"Yep. A Lab I rescued from the animal shelter."

"He's not a Lab," Nana Pat said.

"He looks mostly Lab," Aunt Kat told me. "He's a shaggy mutt and he's perfect."

"He's chaos," Nana Pat said.

"We'll have a playdate!" Aunt Kat practically squealed.

"Gus needs a friend. I'll bring Mervin over to play one day next week."

"Don't you dare," Nana Pat said, but neither one of us was listening to her.

And then Nana Pat cocked her head. She looked a little like Gus, though I knew better than to tell her that. We all got quiet to listen to the sound coming in from outside. Even Gus stopped panting so loud.

"A lawn mower?" Aunt Kat asked.

"No." There was something like awe and wonder on Nana Pat's face. She went to the window and looked out into the backyard. "It's a saw."

She turned around, and she and Aunt Kat gave each other a look that was practically an entire conversation in a language I didn't yet speak.

"Jack's working in his shop," Nana Pat said. Her voice wavered the tiniest bit.

Aunt Kat only gave a pleased little nod.

"I better head home," Aunt Kat said about an hour later. I'd spent the entire time sitting on the kitchen rug with Gus and listening to Aunt Kat and Nana Pat tackle their neighbors' problems and the town's problems and the state's problems. They even had a few national and world problems all worked out. And by the time they'd run out of coffee, I'd heard about the time Aunt Kat had put salt in the sugar bowl and Nana Pat had taken all the elastic out of her grandma's underwear to make a jump rope.

"Glory's probably tired of hearing old family stories," said Aunt Kat.

I'd never had family stories before. I tucked them away, hoping there would be more later.

"Glory, can you carry that bag of vegetables out to her car?" Nana Pat said.

Aunt Kat flapped her hand. "I can do it."

"I don't mind." I picked up the bag. It was heavy. Nana Pat had more vegetables than any of us could eat.

"You have to stay here," I told Gus.

He howled in protest. Sassy pants.

I followed Aunt Kat outside.

"It sure was nice seeing you again," she said.

"You too." It was nice meeting her, since I really didn't remember her all that much from before.

She opened her passenger door. "Just put them on the floorboard." She smiled at me as I straightened up. It was a kind smile, her face jolly, her eyes crinkled, her face showing the memory of all her laughter. She looked like someone who could help.

"Have you talked to my mom?" I blurted out. If Mom hadn't wanted to ask her parents for help, maybe she'd asked Aunt Kat. Maybe she at least knew where she was.

Aunt Kat's face fell. "Oh, sweetie, no, I haven't talked to your mom for a really long time."

"Were you mad at her too?"

Aunt Kat led me to the porch swing that hung from a huge oak tree in the front yard. The swing was weathered and worn and didn't look like it got much use anymore. She sat and patted the wood next to her, so I sat too.

"I wasn't mad at your mom," she said. "I loved her. Love her," she amended when she saw my face. "But we weren't close. I lived in North Carolina the whole time she was growing up, and she was gone to Baton Rouge by the time I moved back to Sweet Olive. The last time I saw your mama was the last time I saw you."

"Why didn't you ever call her?" Maybe Mom wouldn't have left if she hadn't felt so alone. She'd obviously needed help and didn't think she had anyone she could turn to.

I felt mad just then. And sad, for my mom. And angry that she hadn't gotten help.

Aunt Kat and Nana Pat had spent the last hour telling all these family stories. But where was that family when Mom had needed them?

Aunt Kat sighed. "I did call, once or twice. A text on her birthday. But she stopped answering, and I stopped trying." She looked away from me. "I shouldn't have. I'm sorry about that. I—" She took a deep breath. "I had a son. He was close to your mom's age. He died. And talking to your mom made me miss him even more."

"Oh. I'm sorry."

"Me too. But I should have been there more for your mom."

It sounded like my mom maybe should have been there

more for Aunt Kat too. When Mom came to get me, we were going to have a family talk. We needed to be there for each other. Life was too tough to go through all alone.

Aunt Kat patted my hand and stood up. "Have your Nana Pat bring you and Gus by the house sometime. Y'all can meet Mervin. And I've got some embarrassing photos of your grandma I've just been dying to show someone."

"I will."

"I'm glad you're here," Aunt Kat said, pulling me in for another hug. "I know Pat thinks she and Jack are watching out for you this summer, but you and I both know you're keeping an eye on them too. Lord knows they need someone to."

I wasn't exactly sure what she meant.

I took Gus into the backyard when I got back inside. He had been a very good boy during the stories, listening at first, then snoring in a respectful sort of way, without being so loud he interrupted all the juicy parts of the stories. He needed some time to sniff and explore and run off some energy.

Edna Gill's cat streaked by just outside the fence, and Gus bayed and took off, chasing the cat all the way to the corner before he had to stop. He sat down, tipped his head back, and howled in frustration.

"Is that mean old cat teasing you?" I asked.

He gave me what could only be a bloodhound version of a dirty look and began pacing along the fence.

I went to see Papaw Jack, who was still in his shop. I slipped inside the open door. Several overhead lights were on, but it still looked dark until my eyes adjusted from the sunlight. It smelled like oil and dirt and cut wood inside.

"Papaw Jack?" I called out. "Can I come in?"

"Sure!"

I blinked and Papaw Jack took shape. He was standing behind a workbench. A large fan blew hot air around the room, and his hair stuck up. It made him look surprised.

"Sorry about the mess," he said. Cobwebs and dust coated almost every surface. The windows were grimy, and dirt dauber nests clung to the walls in several places. "Shame I let this place get so bad."

"How long since you've worked in here?" By the look Nana Pat had given Aunt Kat, it must have been a while.

"Too long."

"What are you working on now?" I leaned over, but it just looked like wooden stakes to me. "Edna Gill turn out to be a vampire instead of a tomato thief?"

Papaw Jack laughed. It was almost that loud laugh he'd had when I was little. Almost. "They're tracking stakes," he said. "I've got some flagging over there and we're going to tie it to the top."

My throat felt thick for some reason I didn't understand. "Tracking stakes? For Gus?"

He shrugged his left shoulder. "For you." He winked at me. "Nana Pat was fussing at the dishwasher last night because it bent some of her forks."

My face flushed. "Thanks for not spilling the secret."

"Figured we'd both have gotten in trouble." He pointed to the stakes. "Grab those. I'll get the flags."

We carried them to a shaded bench near the garden. "You'll have to tie," he said. He looked hot and tired, but also maybe a little happy. He held the tape down with his right fist and tore it with his left. "Make a strong knot at the top."

We worked our way through all the stakes, and before long, Gus and I had our very own tracking stakes. It felt real now, what we were doing. Not like we were playing, or pretending to find things, but actually learning how to track.

Papaw Jack had spent a lot of time making these stakes for me and Gus. I watched Gus prance and romp around the backyard and thought about how many more stories Aunt Kat and Nana Pat had. I'd thought for so long that I didn't have much family. And now it was starting to feel like I did.

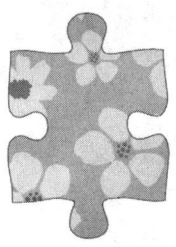

CHAPTER TEN

I called Dad a couple of days later. "Glory Bee!" he shouted when he picked up. Dad was always enthusiastic when he said my name. And now that Papaw Jack had told me the story of that name, I wondered—where was my dad during all that?

"Hey, Dad. Um—were you at the hospital the day I was born?"

Highway noise filled the space between my question and his answer. "I was in Florida. I even tried to get your mom to name you Tallahassee, but by the time I'd gotten home, you already had a name."

I was sure glad Papaw Jack had been the one to pick out my name. His story was a lot better too.

"I drove all night to get there, though."

Gus began barking. It was his I-want-to-chase-something bark, which sounded a lot like a gargling rooster. I opened the door and he tore off into the backyard. The squirrel he was after was at the top of the tree before Gus even made it down the steps.

"What in the world was that?" asked Dad.

"Gus. He's a bloodhound."

"A dog made that sound?"

"Yep."

"When did your Nana Pat get a dog?" He sounded just as shocked as Aunt Kat had.

"He's mine."

"What?"

"Well, just for a little while. I'm babysitting him for a man who is in the hospital."

"Huh. So, I guess that means you're having a pretty good summer."

"Yeah." Gus made everything better. If I were still in Baton Rouge, I would just be alone in our apartment all day. Mom didn't let me have people over when she wasn't home, and since there weren't any kids my age in our apartment building, that meant I spent most of my time by myself, reading or working on puzzles or watching the few channels that came with our cable. But here, I had Gus to keep me company. "I'm training him to track." I explained all about what I was doing and how natural bloodhounds were at it. "They're very good at finding people who've gotten lost."

"And you think you can do all of that before he goes back home?" Dad asked.

"I can try. And Gus is having a lot of fun." As was I.

"I'm glad. You know, I was about your age when I got my first dog. Baxter. I found him in the woods behind our trailer one day after school."

Dad never talked about when he was a kid. Mom had told me that Dad grew up real poor, that his dad left when he was just a boy, but Dad hadn't ever told me much at all. I got still, like any sudden movement might scare him off.

"He was scared and skinny, but he followed me home and I fed him up. My mom was so mad at me when she got home from work. Said she could barely afford to feed us kids. She couldn't afford to feed a dog. But I was already in love with him by then."

I understood that. I had loved Gus the moment I laid eyes on him.

"He was full of ticks and his ribs were showing, but I thought he was the best thing I'd ever seen. I told her I'd buy his food. Take care of him. And I think she was just too tired to argue with me. So I got to keep him. I did odd jobs on the weekends to pay for his food. Fed him scraps when we had them. Baxter followed me everywhere. He was my best friend."

I watched Gus through the window. Yes, I knew that feeling well.

"Man, I hadn't thought about Baxter in a very long time."

"What happened to him?" I asked.

"He died. The year I graduated high school. That's the thing about dogs—they'll break your heart."

I knew that heartbreak was coming. Gus would go home to Mr. Babin and I would be alone again.

That was part of the reason I didn't have any really close friends. It was easier to keep people at arm's length—that way it didn't hurt when they disappointed you. I had learned that young. Mom missed school events, Dad was always gone, and Nana Pat and Papaw Jack stopped visiting, stopped inviting me to stay.

But Gus had needed me. So I'd given him my heart, even though I knew it was probably going to get broken. But it wouldn't be his fault. Dogs were loyal. They never made fun of the holes in your shoes or told you their mom said they couldn't play with you. Dogs stayed.

Until they didn't. But I didn't want to think about that. Not yet.

This might have been the first time Dad had ever talked about something real. I liked this version of Dad. I liked his truths. I wished he would share more of them.

"Have you heard from Mom?" I asked.

Dad coughed. "No. You?"

"Not yet." Her phone was still disconnected. I'd tried calling again last night.

"Well, I'm going to have to let you go, Glory Bee. I've been running this truck through the night, and it's time for a little sleep while everyone else is stuck in rush-hour traffic."

"Okay." I hadn't exactly expected him to talk about Mom, but since he'd finally told me something real, I had been hoping for it.

"I'm glad you called. Talk to you soon." He hung up.

I went outside to find Gus. He'd given up chasing squirrels and was lying in the shade. Edna Gill's face popped up over the fence. It looked like the way a bee sting felt. "That dog has been harassing my cat."

"I'm sorry," I said, though I thought *harassing* was taking it a bit far. "He's a dog who likes to bark."

She narrowed her eyes. "He looks like a dog who likes to bite."

"He would never!" I said. He was big and loud, but nothing about Gus said mean. I'd been reading a lot about bloodhounds, and they were not mean.

"My cat is missing," she said, and her angry face slipped just a little, showing quite clearly how worried she was. She loved her cat like I loved Gus. I would be upset if he were missing too. I felt a little sorry for Edna Gill right then. "And it's that dog's fault."

"Gus wouldn't hurt your cat. If he leaves this backyard, he is on a leash."

Maybe she should keep her cat from jumping our fence. But I didn't say that.

"If he didn't hurt Judy, then he scared her so much she ran away."

"Maybe put a can of tuna out," I suggested. That was what the cat lady at our apartment always did.

"I'll be speaking to your grandma," Edna Gill said. And she walked away.

"I know you didn't do anything to Judy," I told Gus. "Not to hurt your feelings or anything, but you aren't quite athletic enough to catch her." And even if he did chase her, even if he was having a very good day and she was having a very bad one, I truly didn't think Gus would hurt the cat. He loved to chase, but I didn't think he would chomp. I didn't want Nana Pat to have any reason to send Gus away. "We better keep an eye out for Judy, though."

My phone buzzed. *Come to the park?*

It was Rosemary. "Do you want—" Gus jumped to his feet. It didn't matter what I was going to say. Gus always wanted.

I ran in, grabbed his leash, and let Papaw Jack know where I was going. Nana Pat was already at work.

Edna Gill scowled at us as we walked past. Gus didn't even notice.

We'd barely stepped foot in the park when Sebastian ran over. He was grinning and bouncing, a very different boy from the one we'd first met. He was clutching his red stuffed crab.

"Where have y'all been?" he asked, squatting down and petting Gus. He showed Gus his toy. "This is Baby Frab." Gus gave it a polite sniff, then locked in on a smear of jelly on Sebastian's face and promptly removed it for him. Sebastian giggled. "We've been waiting all day."

"It's barely ten," I said.

"He's been up since five at least," Rosemary said as she joined us. "I know because he woke me up too." She glared affectionately at him.

"I've been up since five too!" shouted Lydie. "And I had Pop-Tarts with jelly for breakfast."

I wrinkled my nose. "With jelly?"

Rosemary rolled her eyes. "They eat sugar for breakfast if Mom and Dad aren't around to stop them."

Both kids ran laps around us. Gus turned in a couple of circles and then finally sank into a sit with a huff. Even he couldn't keep up with that kind of energy.

Lydie bounded over. "Let's play hide-and-seek."

"Glory doesn't want to play hide-and-seek," Rosemary said.

"I don't mind. Hide-and-seek is Gus's favorite game."

Lydie stuck her tongue out at Rosemary.

"Though he's probably better at seeking than hiding," I said. Gus had a very large behind for a dog. And he didn't quite understand the concept of sitting still. "I'm training him to find lost people."

"That's really cool," said Rosemary.

I felt like I'd just stepped into the sunshine. That might have been the first time someone my own age told me I was cool.

"Jason sometimes tells us to get lost," Sebastian added.

"Well, if you do, Gus will find you," I told him.

"Jason doesn't really mean it," Rosemary told Sebastian.

Lydie looked doubtful, but I had to agree with Rosemary. When someone decided to get lost, it was really awful on the people left behind.

"You're it!" Lydie hollered at Gus, and the three of them scattered.

I dropped down and touched my forehead to Gus's. I counted to thirty before standing back up. "Ready or not!" I shouted.

Gus gave a loud bark and immediately pulled me over to a tree. Lydie squealed and clapped her hands as Gus stuck his nose in her face, and she planted a kiss on the side of his neck. She took my hand as if we'd always known each other and came along as we rooted out Sebastian and Rosemary.

Gus found Sebastian within five minutes, but he couldn't find Rosemary, who eventually dropped out of a tree and landed gracefully on her feet.

"I'm hungry," Lydie whined after we'd played several rounds.

"Want to come over for lunch?" Rosemary asked me.

"Are you sure it's okay?" I asked.

"Of course."

I followed her through the trees at the back of the park and into her neighborhood. Rosemary's house was painted light blue. Navy shutters hung at the windows. Toys and bikes littered the grass in the front yard, which was patchy and looked like it was often stomped on by a multitude of feet. We climbed the three steps to the front porch, and Rosemary opened the front door.

"Can Gus come in?" I asked.

"No one will even notice," she assured me.

It had been a long time since Emma Mitchell's birthday party. That was the last time I'd been invited to someone's house. Mom said she couldn't afford to buy me stuff, much less other people's kids, so I'd shown up with a dollar-store coloring book wrapped in wrinkled paper.

I'd gone redder than one of Nana Pat's tomatoes when Emma had opened it. She'd made an ugly face, but her mom had made an even uglier one at her, then Emma had told me thank you.

After that, I hadn't wanted to go to any more birthday parties. And eventually, people stopped inviting me.

I had school friends, kids I talked to in class. But I couldn't join clubs or sports or anything that met after school because I had to ride the bus home. I couldn't have people over, so people didn't invite me over. So, while I had school friends, I'd never really been allowed to have life friends.

It was nice, getting invited into someone else's life, especially someone whose life was already so full.

Rosemary's family was big. And loud. And, judging by the living room, a little messy. Nana Pat would have heart palpitations. But I liked it.

Gus did too. So many new smells. He burrowed under a blanket that had been tossed on the floor. He came up chewing.

I rushed over. "What do you have?" I glared at him. He was going to get us kicked out of the house of the only friend we'd made here.

I moved the blanket. Cheese crackers littered the floor. Gus hoovered the rest of them up.

"Thanks, Gus!" Rosemary said. "What other chores can he do?"

"That's about it," I told her.

"Good enough."

We tromped into the kitchen, which was a wreck. Bread, lunch meat, cheese, and mayonnaise were strewn all over the counter. Rosemary rolled her eyes. "Jason. He has football practice in the mornings, which means he's always hungry when he comes home and forgets he lives with other people."

The littles jumped up on stools and waited for her to feed them. I realized Rosemary had a lot of responsibility. She dug around in the fridge and took out jelly.

"Can I help?" I asked.

"I got it. Peanut butter and jelly?" she called out.

"Yep!" Sebastian and Lydie hollered back.

"They eat jelly at every meal, I swear," she said. "Help yourself to whatever is here."

I took Gus over to the rug underneath the kitchen table at the back of the kitchen. "Sit." He sank down. "Stay."

He didn't move when I walked away, but I knew that wouldn't last long. Gus stayed in one place only as long as he wanted to.

I was fixing myself a sandwich when a teenage girl walked in. She was tall and her curly hair was pulled back in a ponytail. "Where have y'all been?" she asked Rosemary.

"At the park," said Rosemary. "I told Jason where we were going."

"I have to run over to Katelyn's. Make sure you clean this mess up when you're done."

"This was Jason's mess to begin with," Rosemary protested, but the girl was already out the door.

"That was Allie," Rosemary said. "My older sister."

There was a beautiful chaos about the kitchen. Artwork and calendars and notes and pictures hung on a bulletin board next to the back door.

Jason and his friends tumbled into the kitchen, grabbing

cookies and handfuls of chips, ruffling the littles' hair. It was like a hurricane of boys blowing through the room, jokes half finished but understood by the rest of them, random words that meant something because they all laughed or responded with other random words. I was willing to bet no one ever felt lonely here—no quiet that seemed to press in on all sides, no eating dinner alone.

Gus couldn't stay away from the noise and movement, not that I could blame him. He pushed and shoved his way into the center of the group, apparently thinking he was one of the boys. He plucked a cookie right out of one of their hands. The boy laughed. "When did y'all get a dog?"

"We didn't," Jason said, petting Gus. "I don't think."

I spoke up. "He's my dog." For now, at least.

"Cool. What kind?"

"A bloodhound." They just seemed to accept me as part of the group. No one asked who I was or questioned my dog being smack-dab in the middle of the kitchen.

One of the boys started to howl. His friends gave him weird looks, then joined in until the kitchen was a chorus of boy noise. Finally, tired of being left out, Gus joined them, throwing his head back and letting out a long and melancholy bay.

The boys cracked up. Lydie and Sebastian grinned, and even Rosemary gave a grudging sort of smile.

"Okay, I'm out," Jason said in Rosemary's direction. "Got to go show these guys what winning's like."

"You wouldn't know winning if it blacked both your eyes," one of them said.

And they were gone, shouting and shoving and ribbing each other all the way down the hall and out the front door.

"What was that all about?" I asked.

"They were off to play video games. No one even asked if they needed to watch these two in case I had something planned today, of course."

"Do you?" I asked.

"No," she said glumly. "But that isn't really the point."

I helped her pick up the kitchen. Gus licked a dish or two before we could get it in the dishwasher. "See?" Rosemary said. "He is good at chores."

"My Nana Pat would have to be hospitalized if she saw Gus licking her dishes."

Rosemary shrugged. "He can't be any germier than Jason. Come on, I'll show you my room."

She put a movie on in Lydie and Sebastian's room. Rosemary's room was right next door.

It was small but absolutely crammed. I felt like I could stand in the center of her room and do a slow spin to learn almost everything I needed to know about this girl. Stacks of books sat next to the bed and along the back wall. A desk, covered in paper and markers and scissors and glitter pens and more books, was underneath the window. And art was tacked up on almost every available space. At first glance I thought all the colorful construction paper was lace, but when I got closer, I realized they were all tiny scenes cut out of paper. I got closer to one, which showed a girl floating through space, surrounded by stars and planets and moons.

"It's called paper cutting," she said, and I could tell she was a little self-conscious.

I turned to look at her. "Did you make that?"

"Yes."

"All of them?"

"All of them."

"Whoa."

She smiled then.

"No, seriously. These are amazing. How did you learn to do that?" I'd never been very good at stuff like that. My teachers had always looked at me funny when I'd turned in my art projects. I usually ended up hacking off about a third of what I was supposed to be cutting out.

"They had a program down at the library," she said. "Two summers ago. The littles were too young to go, so I had the whole afternoon by myself, working on art." Gus made himself at home at the foot of her bed. Rosemary's face took on a dreamy quality as she explained the entire process. She talked about some other artists she liked and showed me a few online accounts of paper cutting.

"Sorry," she said, blushing a little. "I get carried away. You probably don't care about all of that."

"I do!" And I meant it. It was so interesting. "I'm the same way with Agatha Christie. My mom always said people didn't care about all that when I would get to talking too much about her books and Hercule Poirot and how I want to be a detective."

"You do?"

"Yep. I'm going to solve mysteries. Did you know Agatha Christie disappeared? In real life? She wrote mysteries and then was in one. She turned back up eventually, though."

"Cool."

Most people thought she was at some hotel. People needed resets sometimes. Like Mom. When she got her life back on track, she would come back for me.

"So, when is your mom coming home from vacation?" Rosemary asked.

For a second, I worried that I'd just said some of that out loud. But then I realized Rosemary was just curious. I couldn't be upset about that. I was curious too.

"Not until the end of the summer." If Hercule Poirot had been watching me, he'd have known I wasn't telling the complete truth. I looked away from Rosemary's face and shuffled my feet. A good detective probably would have noticed that my heart beat a little faster too.

But Rosemary believed me. "Oh, good. That means we can hang out all summer." She blushed again. "I mean, if you want to."

Except for Gus, I'd never really had anyone who wanted to hang out with me all the time. "Yeah. I do."

My eyes wandered to the paper cuttings she had tacked up. "Can you show me how you do that?"

Her eyes lit up. "Sure!"

She pulled a stool out of the back of her closet and climbed on top. She handed me down a few worn-out board games, then stood on her tiptoes and reached into the very back of the top shelf and pulled down a plastic box. The lid was taped on. She took it over to her desk and pried the top off. "These are really sharp," she said, showing me the silver craft knives. "You have to hide things from Sebastian and Lydie. Like knives and candy."

She disappeared back into the closet and emerged with another plastic box, this one filled with Reese's Pieces and Twizzlers and gummy bears. Gus perked up at that.

"You can't have any of this, buddy," I told him, holding out my hand so that Rosemary could tip some Reese's Pieces into it. "Sorry."

He stood hopefully next to me while I chewed. I showed him my empty hands. He cuddled up to Rosemary, who had stuck a Twizzler in the corner of her mouth. "Sorry, Glory said no," she mumbled around the candy.

Gus flopped to the floor in a huff.

For the next half hour Rosemary showed me how she created the paper art. She chatted while she worked, talking about her school, her family. "Allie thinks she's an adult already and too big for us now," she said. She rolled her eyes and tried to sound thoroughly put out by her ridiculous sister, but I thought she just sounded sad. "Jason is good at every sport so he's always at practice, and he just sort of breezes in and out. But he's really funny and makes the best sandwiches."

"Sandwiches?"

Rosemary looked at me. "Sandwiches. Sometimes he goes into the kitchen and just starts throwing things together. The weirder the better. And the strange thing is that they always taste really good. Like, he somehow knows what flavors go together even if they sound like they don't. And he makes them based on your personality. He's some sort of sandwich genius. He made Sebastian a peanut butter and pepperoni sandwich once."

"That doesn't sound genius," I told her. "It sounds gross!" And like something Gus would love.

"Sebastian loved it. But Jason hasn't done that in a while." She got quiet for a minute.

"Birthdays must be fun." And Christmases. A house full of laughing people sounded amazing. My last birthday had just been me and my mom. She had brought me home a piece of cake from her work, though.

I didn't tell Rosemary any of that. And what would she think if she knew I had no idea where my mom was? Her family was like one from the movies.

"Done!" Rosemary held up the paper. It was very clearly a bloodhound.

"That's Gus!"

She handed it to me. "You can have it."

Rosemary was the coolest. I was so glad Gus had put his nose in someone else's business. "Thanks." I stood up and stretched. "I'd better go." I didn't want to worry Papaw Jack. I suddenly realized Gus was no longer in the room. I immediately imagined him in the trash or chewing on a pair of someone's socks.

I stepped out into the hall and peered into the bedroom next door. Ursula was singing "Poor Unfortunate Souls" on the TV. Lydie and Sebastian were asleep on the floor, both tangled in blankets, Lydie clutching a rather scruffy-looking rabbit, Sebastian with Baby Frab. And Gus was right in the middle of them, flat on his back, all four legs in the air.

That dog. He was the best thing that had ever happened to me.

I hoped I could get him out of the house without waking the other two. From the same amount of time I'd been around this lovely chaotic circus, I knew Rosemary needed some time where she wasn't having to wrestle the two smaller siblings.

I tiptoed into the room and reached down to stroke the side of Gus's neck. His tail twitched, and he blinked his eyes open. "Time to go," I whispered.

He lumbered to his feet. Lydie rolled over but didn't wake up. Sebastian didn't move at all.

"That boy sleeps like a rock," Rosemary said. "One time Mom burned a pie and set off the fire alarm and Sebastian never even twitched." She walked us to the front door and waved as we stepped onto the sidewalk.

"Take us home, Gus," I said.

He didn't take a single detour on the way back.

CHAPTER ELEVEN

Gus and I settled into the rhythm of someone else's house. Nana Pat reported on Mr. Babin's progress. He had come through surgery just fine and was healing. Papaw Jack was working in the garden more and had even started to slowly clean the shop. Gus and I took walks to the park and hung out with Rosemary and Sebastian and Lydie.

Mom didn't call. But I tried not to lose hope.

"I know you can't help the drooling all the time," Nana Pat was saying as I came down the hall. I stopped just outside the kitchen and peered around the doorjamb. She was sitting at the kitchen table with a glass of iced tea. Gus sat in front of her, head cocked as if his ears could better catch her words that way. "But I found some dried drool way up at the top of the kitchen cabinet. How in the world did you get it up there?"

Gus wagged his tail, obviously proud of his talent at somehow beating gravity.

"Maybe you could learn not to shake off in the kitchen. Outside is best. The laundry room in a pinch." She sighed. "Lord knows I've mostly given up in there."

Gus was rather wild with the water drinking. I cleaned up behind him best I could, but he was a pretty accomplished mess maker.

"Speaking of the laundry room, I found a pair of my underwear out in the yard this morning, for all the world to see. Any idea how they got out there?"

Gus pawed her shin. Nana Pat smiled and gave him a pat. "You know, you look like you swallowed a shoe."

Gus had two white ropes of drool on either side of his mouth. They did look like shoelaces. Nana Pat got up and grabbed a couple of paper towels. "If someone had told me I would spend much of this summer wiping a dog's mouth, I would have called them a liar." She wrinkled her nose in disgust as she caught Gus's drool in the paper towel. "Yet here I am."

Gus spied me at that moment and bounded to his feet, throwing his head back and baying a very loud and enthusiastic hello. I'd never walked into a room and had someone so happy to see me. Nana Pat jumped and put her hand on her heart.

"You are the loudest, most dramatic animal I have ever met," Nana Pat told him. I could barely hear her over Gus, who had switched from *Hello* to *Where in the world have you been and why didn't you take me with you?* I was getting fluent in Gus. He was vocal.

I made sure to give him pats and kisses and plenty of attention, even though I'd only been in the shower for ten minutes.

"What are those?" Nana Pat nodded at the stack of books I was holding.

"Library books. Rosemary checked them out for me since I don't have a library card. I need to take them back."

"No kid should go through a summer without a library card," Nana Pat said.

"I've never had a library card."

Nana Pat frowned. I couldn't tell if she was annoyed, disappointed, or angry. I wasn't Hercule Poirot just yet.

She opened the drawer under the phone and took out an envelope. "Let's fix that."

Gus followed us to the door. "You can't go, buddy."

"Oh, he can ride," Nana Pat said. "We won't be inside five minutes. I'll leave the truck running."

I didn't argue with her.

We took Papaw Jack's truck again, which meant I had to boost Gus into the back seat. He rode with his head out the window the whole way there.

Ms. Caroline was behind the desk when Nana Pat and I walked into the library. "Welcome back!" she told me.

"I'm here to get a library card," I said.

"Well, all right." She turned to Nana Pat. "I'll need your driver's license and proof of residence."

Nana Pat pulled that envelope out of her purse and handed everything over. A display with the word *Mystery* over it caught my eye, but I didn't budge as Ms. Caroline typed on the computer. I was getting my very first library card. I wanted to be right here watching it happen.

"Sign here," Ms. Caroline said. Nana Pat signed. I had to sign too. I'd never really had to sign anything before. It felt very official.

Ms. Caroline handed me a plastic card with a drawing of the library on the front. My very own library card. I imagined walking down here and checking out as many books as I wanted to.

"Can I check these out again?" I asked her, setting the bloodhound books on the counter. "This time under my own name?"

"You sure can."

She scanned them and handed them, and my card, back to me.

"I have something for you," Ms. Caroline said.

"Me?"

"Yes, ma'am. Wait right here."

She disappeared into the back and returned a short while later with a paper in her hand. "I saw this the other day and thought of you."

It was a brochure with a bloodhound on the front. He was black and tan, not red like Gus, but he was covered in wrinkles and sniffing at something on the ground. *Tracking Trials* was written across the front.

"I thought you might be interested."

It was a competition for tracking dogs. In October. I would be gone. Gus would be back with Mr. Babin.

But I couldn't stop my heart from wanting it oh so very much.

I stuck the brochure inside the book on the top of my stack. "Thank you." It was easier to be grateful than to explain all the reasons Gus and I wouldn't be able to enter.

I had no idea where I was going to be in the fall. Thinking

about it was hurting more and more as the summer went on. And guilt snuck up behind that want.

Maybe I wasn't allowed to want so much. Not while my mom was struggling to put her life back together.

But I couldn't stop that want from slipping in between everything else.

A car honked outside. And kept honking. And then someone was absolutely laying on that horn.

Ms. Caroline and Nana Pat looked out the front door and I gathered up my books.

"Gus says it's time to go," said Nana Pat.

I ran to the front door. Gus was sitting behind the wheel of the truck. He was honking the horn and howling at the same time.

Gus was talented. I had no doubt we could pass that tracking trial if we entered. He was also an absolute drama queen.

"You are so impatient," I told Gus as we drove away from the library. He licked my ear. I was pretty sure that meant he was glad I was back.

Papaw Jack and I spent most evenings working on the puzzle. Gus usually lay under the table. Tonight, Nana Pat joined us in the den. She examined the puzzle in silence for a minute. "Looking good," she said. She sat in a poufy chair in the corner near us and began working in a workbook with a pencil. After a few minutes, Gus got up so that he was lying halfway between us and Nana Pat.

"What are you working on?" I asked her.

"Logic puzzles."

I perked up. I didn't know Nana Pat liked puzzles. I actually didn't think she could get still long enough to do one. "What's that?"

"Oh, you know, when they give you a bunch of clues and you have to figure out which man lives in which house and what color it is." At my blank expression, she shook her workbook. "Come see."

I got up and leaned over the book. Rows of clues were listed at the top of the page, and then a grid of boxes was at the bottom. "I put Xs when I know it's not a match and checks when I do."

"It's like little mysteries!" I was delighted.

Nana Pat smiled. "I guess it is. I'll pick you up one next time I'm at the store."

I went back to my puzzle. "Thanks!"

"Have you ever seen *Murder, She Wrote?*" Nana Pat asked.

"No." I'd never even heard of it.

"It's this show that came on in the eighties. It's about a mystery writer who solves murders."

"Really?" It sounded cool. "I didn't know you were into mysteries."

"Who doesn't like a good mystery?" she asked.

Exactly.

We all worked in silence for a while. Nana Pat must have finished her puzzle, because eventually she closed her workbook and looked up. "How's the training going?"

"Gus is an expert at finding treats." Besides playing hide-and-seek with Rosemary's crew, those were the only things he had found.

Gus's ears perked up at the word *treat*.

Nana Pat's mouth twisted. "I'll bet he is. Heard he got after Edna Gill's cat."

That old tattletale. "He did not hurt her cat."

"I told her that."

"You did?" I was surprised Nana Pat had defended Gus. She was usually fussing him.

"He's too slow."

I was pretty sure Gus was not following our conversation, but he looked offended all the same.

"He can tell us the boogeyman is on the place, but I doubt he could catch him," Nana Pat said.

"Nana Pat caught a boogeyman one time," Papaw Jack said as he fitted a piece of the puzzle into place.

Nana Pat scowled at him. "Now, there's no need for you to tell that story."

Papaw Jack looked fit to burst, his smile barely contained, nothing but trouble twinkling in his eyes. "Then you better tell it."

She stared at him for a second, then shrugged. "Fine. You'll just exaggerate anyway."

Gus sighed and flopped fully out on his side at Nana Pat's feet, as if settling into the story. I stopped looking for the piece I'd been hunting for and watched Nana Pat instead.

"This happened before we moved to this house," Nana Pat said. "We were just married, and very young. Papaw

Jack went with his buddies on a fishing trip the whole weekend." Her voice was accusing even after all these years.

Papaw Jack held up his left hand. "You said I could go."

"You didn't need my permission. But I was scared to sleep alone in that house."

"You didn't tell me that," he said.

"I know." She looked at me. "I'd never been alone like that before. I'd lived with my parents, and then in college I'd lived in the dorm. I had never slept completely alone in a house before, and I was jumpy."

I had a hard time imagining Nana Pat afraid of anything.

"It was dark. I heard a noise. I looked out the window and saw a man in the backyard."

I gasped. She was sitting right in front of me, so it had obviously turned out all right, but I was scared for her.

"A boogeyman," Papaw Jack said.

"What did you do?" I asked.

"I thought about hiding at first. That's what I wanted to do. But then I would have been scared all night. And I realized it was my house. And no one else should have been there. So I went into the garage and grabbed the Weed eater."

"The Weed eater?"

Nana Pat chuckled. "It was the closest thing I could get my hands on."

"And?" I asked.

"And then I rushed into the backyard and beat that man with the Weed eater."

"While hollering like a banshee," Papaw Jack added.

"Are you telling this story or am I? You weren't even there."

Papaw Jack winked at me. "Neighbor told me. Said it was the scariest thing he'd ever heard."

Now *that* I believed.

Papaw Jack laughed. It was the best sound—there was that reckless laugh of his I remembered.

"What did the man do when you hit him?" I asked Nana Pat.

"Nothing." Nana Pat looked both tickled and embarrassed. "I'd just beaten up one of Papaw Jack's shirts that I'd forgotten on the clothesline."

The den filled with laughter, and Gus blinked up at us, trying to see what was so funny.

The next morning Gus and I went for a walk early. It hadn't taken me long to learn that Gus moved through the world by smell. When he had his head down and was sniffing his way forward, all that loose skin on his face tumbled down and mostly covered his eyes. When he was snorting and shuffling and smelling, it was harder for him to see and hear. In those times, I had to be his eyes. Gus taught me to pay better attention to the world because if I didn't, he might blunder out into the street or fall into a ditch or, as he did five minutes into our walk while I was thinking about Nana Pat using a Weed eater to fight a shirt, walk headfirst into a mailbox.

"Are you okay?" I rubbed the top of his head. Luckily he had a very hard head. He seemed to barely notice what he'd done.

Walking Gus helped me to sort through everything in my head. And there was a lot in there to sort.

My mom had just had the worst year of her life and I hadn't even known it. She'd gotten fired. Couldn't find a new job. Gotten evicted. Run out of money.

And here I was having the best summer I'd ever had. For the first time, I had a dog, and a best friend, and a library card.

I didn't deserve to be this happy.

I missed Mom, and I was still angry that she hadn't thought she could trust me with the truth, that she'd left me behind.

But I hoped she had a better job and apartment now. And when she came back for me, I was going to be a much bigger help. And she was going to be so proud of me when I told her all about training Gus.

I'd read over the tracking-trial brochure three times last night before I'd gone to bed. The competition was in Mead in October. Maybe, if Mr. Babin was feeling better, he could enter Gus. I knew Gus could pass. He was so smart.

I told myself the whole point of training Gus had been to make Mr. Babin happy. But the fact was, I wanted to track with Gus.

Everything must have smelled extra interesting today, because even though we came this way all the time, Gus was walking slow and sniffing everything. I had to work to keep him on the path. He kept zigzagging, chasing scents.

Gus tugged me off the sidewalk. I tugged back, barely getting him to stop. "No, we're not going that way," I told him. "You can't just clomp through someone's yard." I continued trying to go forward.

Gus came to a dead stop and refused to move. "You changed your mind about the walk?" I asked. "You know, everything I've read has said a well-trained dog listens to his owner." Gus did not really like listening. Gus liked bossing. He was like Nana Pat in that regard.

He tugged me again off the sidewalk and toward a bunch of trees growing between yards.

I huffed. I was starting to sound a little bit like Gus. "Fine. But then we go where I want to go."

The minute I turned toward the trees, Gus was off. I had to trot to keep up with him. "Do you smell something, boy?" Because he was on a trail.

He barreled through the trees and undergrowth. I hoped we weren't going to get in trouble for trespassing. He slowed down some the deeper we got into the shade, and his head went down. I could hear his nose working. He turned his head right and left, and his ears flopped and flapped, maybe giving him clues, because he followed a twisting trail.

Maybe this was a bit of no-man's-land like the abandoned park, because there was trash tangled up in the leaves and an old tire sitting at the base of a dead tree.

Gus pulled me over to the tire.

"Oh," I said when I realized what he'd found. "You are a very good boy."

Edna Gill's cat, Judy, was lying inside the old tire. She was surrounded by kittens!

She glared at Gus, but she was obviously too tired to protest. Gus sniffed and sniffed and wagged his tail, but he didn't try to get too close, only smelled and then looked up at me as if to say, *See, I knew what I was doing all along.*

"There'll be no living with you after this, will there?" I asked him. I thought maybe there was a smug look under all those wrinkles. He wagged his tail and leaned over the tire for a closer look. "You were right." I counted the kittens. "Six babies? You are a very good mama," I told her, and for some reason, that made my chest a little tight. "We're not going to bother you or your babies, I promise. But I think maybe you'd be happier if you were at home."

I tugged Gus away from his find. "We have to go tell Mrs. Gill."

Now that he had thoroughly investigated the scent, Gus consented to go with me fairly easily.

"I am so proud of you," I told him. "Proving your innocence, huh? Very smart."

I was sweaty by the time we climbed the steps of Edna Gill's front porch and knocked on her door. Gus sank into a sit, panting. "Good boy," I whispered.

Edna Gill opened the door only a crack, making it quite clear Gus and I were not going to be invited inside.

I got straight to the point. "Gus found Judy."

"Oh!" She put her hand on her chest.

"He didn't hurt her!" I assured Mrs. Gill. "Judy and her

six kittens are just fine." Mrs. Gill's mouth opened and closed. I grinned. "You didn't know she was going to be a mama?"

Mrs. Gill shook her head, then seemed to pull herself together. "She's really okay?"

"She's fine. We can show you where she is."

Mrs. Gill was smiling now. "Kittens. Who knew? You stay right here—I'll be right back."

She shut the door, leaving us on the front porch. Gus sniffed all her flowerpots. "Don't pee on any of them," I warned him. We'd just gotten on Mrs. Gill's good side.

Mrs. Gill wasn't long at all, coming back to the door with a laundry basket lined with towels. "How far is it?" Her eyes flitted between her car and Gus. I knew what she was thinking.

"Not far. We'll walk and you can follow us in the car."

And that was what we did. She drove slowly right behind us as we walked along the sidewalk, then she parked on the street and carried the laundry basket into the trees.

"Judy, baby," Mrs. Gill crooned when she caught sight of her cat and her new family. Judy meowed very loudly, and soon the kittens joined in with loud, high-pitched mews that had Gus cocking his head and pacing, curious about what the tiny, loud balls of fluff were.

I hoped Mrs. Gill noticed that Gus didn't try to taste a single one of them.

She turned to me once she'd gotten Judy and her kittens settled into the back seat. "Thank you."

"It was all Gus."

Mrs. Gill's face no longer looked like a bee sting felt. She gave Gus a tentative pat on the top of the head. "Thank you too."

Gus said *You're welcome* by drooling on her shoe.

CHAPTER TWELVE

The doorbell rang on Friday. "I got it!" I shouted, though nobody heard me over Gus's noise. He ran toward the door, howling out his happiness at having a visitor. Sometimes I wished I was as confident as Gus was, that I could holler out whatever emotion I was feeling, but I knew better. Babies and dogs could shout. The rest of us had to train our emotions to follow the rules.

But I was just as excited as Gus, since this visitor was for me. I grabbed hold of Gus's collar and opened the door.

Rosemary and her mom were standing on the front porch. Rosemary was carrying an overnight bag. I hadn't ever met Rosemary's mom before. She was softer than Rosemary, her eyes round with surprise at Gus's noise.

"Come on in," I said, "before Gus gets out." He was desperately trying to get to Rosemary.

They hurried inside and shut the door. Rosemary decided she'd better give Gus some attention, since he was barking and howling and stomping and genuinely being a rather intense door greeter. "Hi, Gus," Rosemary said, giving him a good pat. "I'm glad to see you too."

"I'm Deanna," Rosemary's mom said. "I have been dying to finally meet Gus and Glory. That's all my kids talk about these days."

Rosemary blushed and rolled her eyes. "Mom."

Deanna laughed and waved her hand, pushing aside Rosemary's obvious embarrassment.

Gus, having thoroughly inspected Rosemary, moved on to her mom. He sniffed her shoes and wiped his mouth on her jeans.

"I've heard a lot about you," she told Gus. "Even from Jason, who barely notices anything if it's not a football or video game." She straightened up. "Are your grandparents home?"

"My Papaw Jack is in the den, and Nana Pat is at work but will be home soon."

Papaw Jack shuffled out of the den and waved hello with his left hand.

"Thanks for letting Rosemary stay over," Deanna told him.

"Any time."

I watched Rosemary's mom. She didn't flinch at Papaw Jack's gravelly voice. I decided I liked her.

"Hope they don't give you too much trouble."

Rosemary rolled her eyes again, but Papaw Jack just smiled. "I have backup."

If Gus was in charge, we were all in trouble.

"Well, I'd better go. I promised the littles I'd bring home ice cream." She turned to Rosemary and lowered her voice. "Remember your manners."

"Yes, ma'am." But Rosemary practically pushed her mom out the door. She was scowling a little when she turned back to me. "She treats me like I'm practically an adult when she needs me to babysit and like a kid when she doesn't need something." She shook her head in frustration, then let her scowl slide off her face. "Notice anything different about me?"

Gus cocked his head, as if he were trying to figure it out.

She hadn't cut her hair. Her shoes were dirty, so they couldn't be new. I was supposed to be a detective—this was supposed to be easy. But before I could finish categorizing what was the same so that I could see what was different, she told me. "I'm alone!" Her excitement seemed a bit disproportionate to the event. I almost pointed out that she couldn't be alone if I was standing right in front of her, but I knew what she meant.

"It makes you look shorter," I said.

She laughed and gave me a light shove.

"Come on. Let's put your stuff in my room. Then you can meet my grandpa." He'd disappeared into the den to give us space.

Gus plodded up behind us, obviously afraid to miss out on any adventure. Rosemary gave a little gasp as I opened the door, and I jumped back, alert for danger. Detectives always should be. But Rosemary was smiling. "It's huge! And look at those round windows!"

And even though this wasn't my forever room, I felt proud.

"You hung up the picture!"

"Of course." I'd put her paper cutting of Gus next to the

postcards from Dad. I'd gotten another one just yesterday from Wyoming. It had a picture of the world's largest jackalope on it.

"Have you been to all these places?" she asked.

"No. Those are from my dad. He's a truck driver."

"That's cool. Where is he now?"

"Last I heard he was in Oregon."

"Wow. I've only been to Texas, Mississippi, Alabama, and Florida. It's expensive taking five kids on vacation."

I knew all about not being able to afford things. But I didn't admit that I'd never even left Louisiana.

"Is that your mom?" Rosemary pointed to the picture of me and my mom.

"Yes." I was proud of that picture. In that picture my mom looked like someone who stayed. In that picture she had a good job and had never been evicted. In that picture, her arms kept me safe.

The way Mom was smiling at me then made me believe she really was coming back.

"So is your mom in Oregon too?"

I didn't want to talk about Mom. I didn't want Rosemary to know I had no idea where my mother was. Hers dropped her off at sleepovers and picked up ice cream for little siblings. I wanted Rosemary to think I was a girl with a normal family. I didn't want to give her any reason to look at me differently or decide she didn't want to be my friend after all. "No. My parents are divorced."

"Oh. Sorry."

"It's okay. I don't even remember them being married."

I headed to the door. "Let's go see Papaw Jack. He had a stroke, so sometimes he's hard to understand."

She looked serious all of a sudden. "Got it."

Papaw Jack turned the TV off when we came in. Gus immediately flopped down at his feet.

"Papaw Jack, this is my friend Rosemary. She lives over by the park."

Papaw Jack got to his feet. "Nice to meet you, Rosemary," he said. He slowly enunciated every word to make sure she understood.

"Nice to meet you too!" Rosemary shouted.

I gave her a quick jab with my elbow. "He just talks slow," I reminded her. "He's not deaf."

Rosemary blushed a shade of red that was almost frightening. "I'm sorry," she said.

Papaw Jack flapped his left hand and sat back down in his chair. "No sorrys for using your voice."

Rosemary looked at his face like he had said the most brilliant thing she'd ever heard. "Huh," she finally said. She whispered to me. "I like him."

I smiled. Me too. It was really nice getting to know him this summer.

"Have you read all of these books?" Rosemary asked Papaw Jack. She was looking with wonder at the colorful spines.

"Not all, but most," he said.

"I like to read. Mostly books about dragons." And she launched into a summary of the one she was reading. It sounded pretty good, even if it didn't have any detectives in it.

Papaw Jack listened. He nodded, and once or twice he asked a question. Rosemary looked thrilled that she was able to get through so many sentences without being interrupted.

"Want a snack?" I asked Rosemary once she was finished. "I think there are Popsicles in the freezer."

"Want to know a secret?" Rosemary asked. "I'm pretty much always hungry."

"Like Gus," Papaw Jack told her.

Gus, loyal and true, followed Rosemary and me into the kitchen, hoping he was going to get a snack too.

He was. I hadn't yet learned how to tell that mournful face no. I dug around in the freezer and came up with three Popsicles.

"Your grandpa is a very good listener," Rosemary said as we went into the backyard.

"He really is."

We sat in the shade. Gus ate his Popsicle in two large bites, but Rosemary and I took a little bit longer. We talked about TV shows we'd seen and books we liked. Rosemary liked the fanciful and I liked the real, but I promised her I would read her dragon book if she read an Agatha Christie.

"Now what?" I asked. "Are there sleepover rules or something?"

"You've never had a sleepover?"

"Mom worked a lot," I said. "And we didn't always live in the nicest apartments." One girl in second grade told me that her mom said she couldn't stay the night because we didn't live somewhere safe.

So, I wanted to do everything right on my very first sleepover.

"No rules. That's the great thing about sleepovers!" She grinned. "And no little siblings either."

"Well, there is Gus," I said.

"Yeah, but he's cool."

He had all four legs in the air and was letting the sun warm his belly. "He's definitely something."

"Since you've never had a sleepover, you decide," Rosemary said. "It's your house anyway."

Was it? It no longer felt like just the place where I stayed. But it wasn't a true home either. Eventually, I was going to have to leave.

"Let's go visit Mrs. Gill's kittens," I said.

Rosemary clasped her hands together and looked delighted. "Oh, yes please!"

"Do you want to visit the floof babies?" I asked Gus.

He rolled over and looked extremely serious.

"Are you sure?" Rosemary asked. She cast a wary eye toward Mrs. Gill's house.

"She adores Gus now," I assured her. I looked over at his wrinkly face. "How could she not?"

Even though Mrs. Gill had decided Gus wasn't a cat-eating monster, she still wouldn't let him in her house, so she opened the backyard gate and brought the basket of kittens outside. Judy seemed glad for the break. The kittens were just getting big enough to play now.

"They're so fluffy!" Rosemary said. She picked up the

ginger cat and held it against her chest. It snuggled into her shirt.

The rest of them climbed Gus like a mountain. He was really gentle with them, lying on his side and letting them roam all over his wrinkled skin. He rolled his eyes at me once, as if to say, *What can you do?*

"Do you think Mrs. Gill is going to keep all of them?" Rosemary asked.

"I don't think so."

"Maybe my parents will let me have one of them." She was holding a black cat now. He had one white paw. "They're easier than dogs, right?"

"They take up less space, that's for sure," I said, eyeing Gus. Two of the kittens had curled up against his belly and fallen asleep. Both of them were purring.

Nana Pat brought home pizza for dinner. She even let Rosemary and me eat it picnic-style on a huge blanket in front of the TV in the den. We had to shut the sliding doors into the den to keep Gus out of the pizza, and he was supremely offended at being left out. He whined and yowled and smacked the door. Papaw Jack finally took him out into the garden for a little while, though as soon as we'd finished eating, I let him in. He stomped all over the blanket, gave me a dirty look when he realized I hadn't dropped any pepperoni, and flopped down in front of the movie.

Rosemary and I sat on either side of him, and eventually Gus rested his head on my leg, so I knew I was forgiven.

"What would you wish for?" Rosemary asked once the movie was over. It had been about a kid with three wishes. All the wishes went wrong, but it turned out all right in the end.

I didn't have to think hard about that one. And I didn't even need three. I only had two. I wanted my mom to come home and for Gus to be mine forever.

"I don't know," I lied. "What would you wish for?"

"A dragon," she said immediately.

"I definitely think your parents would object to a pet that big."

"Then I would also wish for a castle big enough for a dragon."

"Nice."

We went upstairs and piled on my bed. Gus circled his four or five times before lying down.

"You know," Rosemary finally said, "if I did live in a big castle, I think my parents might forget I even existed."

"What do you mean?"

Rosemary picked at a ribbon on one of the quilts. "I sort of get lost at my house. Allie is the oldest and Jason is the athlete and Sebastian is the sweetest and Lydie is an adorable little tyrant and me . . ." She shrugged. "I'm just stuck in the middle. It's kind of lonely."

I never would have thought that Rosemary could feel alone in a house full of noise and people. But I knew what lonely was.

"Maybe you should make more noise," I told her.

"Huh?"

"That's what Gus does when he wants attention. He makes an absolute racket."

"My house is nothing but racket."

I laughed. "Maybe you should tell your parents how you feel." I would have given anything to be able to talk to my mom.

Rosemary didn't look sold on the idea. "You're lucky," she said. "It's harder for parents to forget about a kid if they have only one."

Harder, but not impossible. That made me feel even worse. My parents only had the one kid, but they lived their lives as if they didn't have any.

I wanted Rosemary to know she wasn't alone. I wanted to know I wasn't alone. And I wanted an actual friend, one I trusted and confided in. "I didn't tell you the whole truth. About my mom," I admitted.

Rosemary didn't say anything, just settled in to show me that she was listening.

"She's not really on vacation. That's what everyone told me, but it's not the truth." I took a deep breath. "My mom left." *Me*, I added to myself. My mom left me.

"Do you know where she went?"

I shook my head. "It's a mystery. One I've been trying to solve."

"Do you think she's coming back?"

"Yes." I tried to sound more certain than I felt. I hesitated, then I leaned over and pulled Mom's dream book out from under the bed. I hadn't shown it to anyone, but Rosemary was my friend. I could trust her. I showed her the pictures. "I think she went to one of these places. And I think once she's settled, she's going to come get me."

Rosemary didn't say anything as she flipped through the book. Finally she looked up. "And you want to move to one of these places?"

I wanted to be with my mom. She wasn't a bad mom or the best mom. She was just Mom.

"I really like Sweet Olive." I wished I could keep Gus and Rosemary and Nana Pat and Papaw Jack and have Mom too. But I didn't think it was going to work out that way.

"But you miss your mom."

"Yeah."

Rosemary, like Papaw Jack, was a really good listener. I thought maybe she'd had to learn that, being in her family. A lot of people meant a lot of talking.

"That has to be a little scary, not knowing what's going to happen."

"It is." I hadn't admitted that to anyone but Gus.

"Well, you have me," she said. "And you know I'm never going anywhere." She made a face about it, but I knew she was mostly joking.

It was nice having a friend. And I had more than just Rosemary.

I had a great-aunt and a library card. I had grandparents who let me have indoor picnics and sleepovers.

The neighbors didn't yell. The electricity didn't get shut off. The landlord didn't bang on the door and holler. And I didn't have to hide in my room when he did because Mom wasn't home and I knew we didn't have the rent and I didn't know what to say.

Mostly, I wasn't lonely here, and I wondered if going back to the way things were would make me feel even lonelier than I ever had.

As much as I missed my mom, I realized I didn't want things to go back to the way they had been. I wanted my new life with Mom to be different. For both of us.

CHAPTER THIRTEEN

Today was the day Gus was going to meet Mervin. I was super excited. One dog was great, but two dogs were even better. Plus, it would be good for Gus to have a friend.

Friends were important. I'd kind of thought for a while that I was just the kind of person who didn't really have close friends. But now that I'd met Rosemary, I realized I just hadn't found my people yet.

This summer, I was meeting my people.

Papaw Jack stayed home instead of going to Aunt Kat's with us. He had an appointment with a physical therapist, who was coming to the house. Apparently, this was a big deal. I'd overheard him and Nana Pat talking about it. It sounded like he'd been refusing to do physical therapy ever since his stroke but, for some reason, had changed his mind.

I was being curious when I overheard this, to be clear. Not nosy.

Once again, Gus had to be helped into the truck. Once again, he hung his head out the window and sang, ears flapping, drool flying. Everyone at the stoplight was smiling at him. Gus was like a slobbering, fuzzy joy fairy.

Aunt Kat lived alone in a cute little house on the other side of town. Nana Pat parked in the driveway, and I walked Gus up to the front door and rang the doorbell.

A dog immediately started barking. Gus woofed deep in his chest. Aunt Kat opened the door.

"Come in if you can get in!" she said, pushing a dog out of the way so we could get inside. "Mervin, sit."

Mervin did.

Mervin looked like someone had started drawing a Labrador and given up halfway through. He was mostly black, but a reddish-brown stripe ran down his bushy tail, which made his back end look like a fox's. His ears stuck up at the bottom and then folded out to the sides at the top, kind of like a paper airplane. He had short legs and the most beautiful yellow eyes.

He loved Gus immediately.

Gus, upon first glance, seemed to be deciding if he was going to tolerate Mervin or pretend he didn't exist. Mervin bounced and twisted and wagged his tail. Gus sniffed. His tail twitched. He sniffed some more. His tail wagged harder.

And then Gus cut to the right and the chase was on. The dogs ran out the open back door and into the backyard, Gus baying, Mervin barking and leaping into the air.

"I think the playdate is a success," Aunt Kat declared.

Aunt Kat and Nana Pat went into the living room, but I followed the dogs outside. Mervin was running circles around Gus, who had decided he had to catalog every new scent in this backyard before he could even think about playing.

Mervin bounded over to me, tongue lolling out of the

side of his mouth. "Hi, Mervin." I scratched his ears, which folded back against his head and mostly disappeared. "It's nice to meet you."

He closed his eyes as I rubbed his head, then flipped around so I could scratch his back. He stomped one of his little legs when I hit the sweet spot.

I laughed. Gus ran over and pushed his body in between me and Mervin. "Are you jealous?" I asked Gus. I rubbed his ears so he wouldn't feel neglected. "Y'all are both spoiled rotten. Go play."

They chased each other. Mervin ran over to make sure I was included. Gus barked at a squirrel. Mervin brought me a ball. "Fetch, Mervin!" I threw the ball and he brought it halfway back. I walked over and got it. "Gus, your turn!" I showed Gus the ball and threw it. Gus ran after it, sniffed it, then walked away, apparently too dignified to fetch a tennis ball.

"You're not too good to drag underwear out of the dirty-clothes basket, though," I reminded him.

Eventually Gus and Mervin wore themselves out. I left them snoozing in the shade and went inside for something to drink.

"But where is she?" Aunt Kat's voice floated out of the living room. She was trying to whisper, but pretty much nothing about Aunt Kat was quiet.

"I don't know, Kat. I really don't. I wish I did. And I wish I could say this wasn't like Layla. But she's spent her life quitting things. Maybe it became all too much and she just quit being a mother."

"You don't ever quit being a mother." Aunt Kat's voice was hard.

"Oh, honey, I'm sorry. You know I know that. I mean she quit mother*ing*."

"But I don't understand how she could have just abandoned her daughter. She was raised better than that."

Nana Pat's voice was full of pain. "Maybe not."

But I couldn't listen to any more.

"She didn't leave me!" I shouted as I stepped into the living room. "Maybe she is on vacation, just like you said. She's in New York or Paris or San Francisco and she's coming to get me." My fists clenched at my sides. "Neither one of you were there for my mom. So you don't get to talk about her like that!"

Aunt Kat and Nana Pat were silent now. Just like every other adult in my life.

I whirled around and stormed back outside. They didn't come after me. Maybe they thought I wasn't worth it.

I wedged myself between Mervin and Gus. Gus grunted and rolled over. Mervin sat up, his back pressed against my side, and seemed to be sitting between me and the world.

Aunt Kat had no idea what she was talking about. Moms didn't just walk away without looking back. Moms came home eventually.

Didn't they?

Did everyone think Mom had abandoned me? Did they think I was unlovable? Too much trouble?

I rested my hand on Gus's side, which was warm from the

sun. Gus loved me. When everyone else had walked away, Gus had found me.

Would Nana Pat send me away now? She and my mom had had a fight and didn't see each other for over a year. Maybe this was my and Nana Pat's fight and she wouldn't want to see me anymore either.

I put my head on Gus's side and listened to his heart beat. His chest rose and fell with each breath.

I didn't want to be sent away from Gus. Gus needed me. And I needed him.

Mervin raced away, and Gus lumbered to his feet and followed. Aunt Kat had come out into the backyard. "I'm sorry," she said. "I shouldn't have said what I said."

"It's what everyone thinks, isn't it? That Mom just left me?"

"Most of us don't know what to think," she said. "But no matter what happens, none of this is your fault. And it's not fair. You should get to be a silly kid."

I didn't believe in the word *should*. Lots of things should have been different. But they weren't.

"Pat is waiting on you in the truck."

I sat in the back with Gus. He fell asleep in my lap. Nana Pat didn't apologize. In fact, she didn't say a single word on the way home. It made me feel even worse than if she had yelled at me.

When we got home, I took Gus outside to practice tracking. Papaw Jack was napping, so I couldn't ask him to hide. I needed to ask Nana Pat, because the book said I should use a bunch of different people to give Gus all the practice, but Nana Pat was obviously mad at me. I was hoping if I stayed mostly still and silent and invisible, she would forget about sending me away until the summer was over.

A girl in my fourth-grade class had been in foster care. She got moved around a lot. If Nana Pat decided I was too much trouble, and Dad didn't want to stay home with me, then I would probably have to go live with strangers. And then Mom would never be able to find me.

I wished I had Rosemary's family. They were big and loud and probably got on each other's nerves, but they were there for each other. Maybe they didn't always listen to her, but Rosemary didn't have to worry about being sent away.

I laid the tracking trail myself, leaving my sock at the end of it. I'd go to the park tomorrow and get Rosemary to hide. Sebastian had a tendency to wander too much, and Lydie never could stay hidden long enough for Gus to follow the full trail. I started in the backyard like always, but I meandered out of the gate and around to the front yard. Gus wouldn't improve if I kept all the trails short and easy.

Gus started off fine, immediately following the trail outside the gate, but once there, the variety of smells he wasn't really used to seemed to throw him off. He veered off and spent a lot of time smelling at the base of a tree. He barked at a squirrel. He pulled me in the opposite direction of all the flags I had meticulously put out to mark where I'd walked. I pulled him back to the trail and reminded him what he was supposed to be doing. "Find it."

He seemed to be interested in finding everything but the trail. It was hot, and I was sweaty, and I was getting frustrated. I took him back to the trail a third time.

When we came into the front yard, Gus bayed long and loud, and I snapped my head up, hoping it wasn't Judy. We didn't need anyone else mad at us.

It wasn't. A brown dog that looked like a sausage waddled past, his owner looking over at Gus in worry. Gus barked and bayed and bounced on his toes, but I knew that just meant he wanted to say hello. The sausage dog seemed to want to say hello too. His little tail was wagging, making his entire back end swing wide. Gus tugged hard on his leash, pulling me closer even though I was trying to stop him, and the woman scooped up her little dog.

"He's not mean," I tried to tell her. "He just likes to visit." But I was pretty sure she couldn't hear a thing over Gus's noise.

"Stop barking!" I told Gus.

He did not stop barking. Gus did exactly what he wanted to do until he didn't want to do it anymore.

"Nobody likes being yelled at," I told him.

And then I immediately felt guilty again for my behavior at Aunt Kat's. Nobody liked being yelled at.

I gave up on Gus finding the treats at the end of the trail. Today had been an utter failure. Maybe I couldn't train him to find anything. I was just a kid who'd never even had a dog before.

A kid whose mom left without even saying goodbye. Without calling to check on her.

Even if Mom was coming back, and I believed she was, it wouldn't have hurt her to call and check in on me. Let me know she was okay. Let me know we would be together soon.

Did she even miss me at all?

I walked Gus back through the gate and inside the fence. I felt small and heavy, like a rain cloud about to burst.

"That bad?" Papaw Jack asked.

I looked up. He was sitting on the bench in the shade.

"I'm sorry Gus woke you up," I said. I was sorry about a lot of things.

"I needed to get up." He patted the bench next to him. I took Gus's leash off and got him some water first. He lapped it up then trailed water back to the bench, where he wiped his mouth on Papaw Jack's leg and flopped to the grass.

I sat on the bench next to Papaw Jack. Neither of us said anything, which didn't feel awkward, since Papaw Jack was quiet most of the time.

"How was Mervin?" he finally asked.

I didn't want to talk about what had happened at Aunt Kat's. My face felt hot. "Mervin loved Gus."

"He's easy to love."

He was. He didn't have to worry about being sent away. Mr. Babin wanted him and I wanted him and Rosemary and her siblings all wanted him around. Even Mrs. Gill liked Gus now. Mostly.

"How was physical therapy?" I asked.

"Long overdue." He looked toward the garden. The squash plants were huge. I'd lived here long enough that now I knew what the plants in the vegetable garden were. "I refused to do it for a long time. But your Nana Pat wouldn't quit fussing about it."

"Why did you change your mind?"

He looked at Gus, who was stretched out on his side. He smiled at me. "It was time." He winked at me. "And to get your Nana Pat to stop fussing."

I tried to smile back, but I couldn't make it work. I kind of hoped she'd fuss at me a little. It would be better than the silence. Mom hadn't said a word to me about wanting to live anywhere else, and then she was just gone, no goodbye.

Sometimes silence hurt way worse than words.

Maybe Papaw Jack understood what was in the silence better than I did, because he said, "You know what's great about stubborn people? They don't give up." Then he patted my leg and went into the house.

I sat on the ground and touched my forehead to Gus's. "Thanks for not giving up on me," I whispered. "I won't ever give up on you either."

After a mostly silent dinner where I felt awful and pushed my food around on my plate, I dragged a blanket outside into the backyard. Being in the house made me feel all closed up, and I wanted to be where I could breathe. Gus and I lay on the blanket and looked up at the stars.

There were more stars here than there were in Baton Rouge. One of them was really, really bright, and a few of them were twinkling. My science teacher had told us once that the atmosphere was what made the stars twinkle, but I liked the idea that they were winking down on me, like me and the stars had our own little secret.

They were there, shining like they had been for years and years, and no matter how sad or scared I was, they were still going to be there tomorrow. It was nice, knowing that some things stayed put, some things didn't run away, some things shone down no matter what.

Gus's breathing was steady. I knew that Gus would have to go back to his own house soon, but right then, it felt like he would always be right by my side, his loud bark scaring off my loneliness.

I ran my hand down his side, and his tail wagged in response. "It's going to be okay," I whispered, to myself more than him. "Everything is going to be okay."

It was a wish I sent up toward the stars. They winked down, my wish heard, my secret safe.

CHAPTER FOURTEEN

The silence in the house the next day was so loud I could barely stand it. Even Gus seemed to notice. I took him for a walk, thinking if maybe I stayed out of Nana Pat's sight, she would forget about sending me away.

Maybe one of my parents would remember they had a daughter and I wouldn't have to worry about having a place to live.

My anger roiled around in my head, but it kept bumping into my worry. That meant I basically had a big ol' storm brewing in my brain.

And Gus somehow sensed it. He marched us straight to the park without any detours. Rosemary was already there.

"Sebastian and Lydie are with Mom," Rosemary said as soon as I walked up. "Sebastian broke his glasses again." She squatted down and loved on Gus. He said thank you by wiping drool in her hair.

"Will you lay a trail for Gus?" I asked her. "Make it a little twisty." He needed more practice.

Rosemary took my training bag and headed to the back of the park. Gus and I kept our backs to her.

"Done!"

The flags fluttered in the breeze. I was glad I wasn't still having to use Nana Pat's forks.

All that storm turned into background noise when I was working with Gus. I wasn't mad or scared. I was just focused.

And today, so was Gus. He found every single treat on his way to the end of the trail.

"Thanks for helping me train Gus," I told Rosemary.

"I'm going to miss it when he goes home," she said.

It felt like another piece of my heart chipped off. Was I going to have any of it left at the end of all this? Maybe I would just have a bunch of jagged pieces of heart rattling around in my chest. I wasn't sure even I could puzzle it back together again.

"Me too."

"I'm sorry," Rosemary said, her eyes roaming my face. "I shouldn't have mentioned it."

"It's okay. It's the truth." And I wasn't going to hide from that like everyone else in my family.

Gus flopped to the ground, panting. Sweat trickled down my back. Summer blazed through Sweet Olive, and the air felt thick enough to slice. I prayed for a breeze, a cloud, a freak snowstorm.

I turned to Rosemary. "Let's go get snowballs."

"You have all the good ideas."

The snowball stand was in a tiny trailer near the library. Rosemary and I got in line. It didn't take long for Gus to get all the attention. Everyone wanted to pet him, and he slobbered and panted and wagged his tail as both kids and adults patted his head and told him how handsome he was.

Before Gus, back when I'd lived with Mom, I'd sometimes wondered if I'd gone invisible. Whole days would go by without another person speaking to me. But no way Gus blended in—he was born for the light.

"Next in line!"

I stepped up and ordered a strawberries-and-cream snowball. "And can you do a cherry snowball, light on the syrup, in a bowl for my dog?"

The teenage boy who was working the stand leaned forward to look at Gus. He grinned. "Absolutely."

Rosemary got a lemonade snowball and we took our orders and sat on a bench in the shade. I put Gus's snowball on the ground, and he immediately began slurping it. I wondered if dogs got brain freezes.

"Gus is getting really good at tracking," Rosemary said.

"He is." I took a bite of my snowball. It was melting faster than I could eat it in this heat. "Ms. Caroline told me about a tracking trial in Mead."

Rosemary's face lit up. "That's awesome!"

I nodded. Watching Gus track, solving the tiny mysteries as he did, was so much fun. Working with Gus was helping me learn to listen to him. I was getting much better at knowing what he wanted and how he was feeling.

But the idea of entering tracking trials and competitions was even more exciting because I wouldn't know the mystery beforehand. Maybe Mr. Babin would be okay with me entering the trial with Gus.

"It's in October," I said.

Rosemary's face fell. "Oh. You'll be with your mom."

The problem was, I didn't know where I would be in the fall. Maybe I'd be in Lafayette with Dad. Maybe I'd be in a whole other state with Mom.

Maybe I would be with strangers.

"And Gus will be back with Mr. Babin."

"But you'll be able to come back and visit, right?" Rosemary asked. "To see your grandparents?"

"I'm not sure they'll want me." I cleared my throat. "Nana Pat is mad at me. We had a fight." Was it a fight if I was the only one who had said anything? She wasn't fighting at all—maybe because she didn't think it was worth the trouble.

"Of course she'll want you to visit. Families fight sometimes. Last night I took your advice and made a racket."

"Really?"

Rosemary looked pretty proud of herself. "I got mad at my dad and told him I wanted to throw his stupid phone in a lake. He still hugged me good night."

But her family and mine were nothing alike.

"Families aren't perfect," she said. "They don't have to be."

But I wasn't sure I even had a family. We were separate people who never really stuck together. We were related—but that didn't necessarily make us family.

A truck pulled into a parking spot next to the snowball stand, and a man hopped out. "Rosemary!"

"That's my dad," she said, looking worried.

Maybe she was in trouble after all.

Her dad strode over to our bench. He looked a lot like Rosemary, all angles and elbows, but he wore glasses like Sebastian. He had an air of forgetfulness about him, though I couldn't say why. Maybe it was the way his hair stuck up a little in the back. Or the fact that his shirt was buttoned crooked at the bottom.

"My meeting finished early," he told Rosemary, "so I thought I'd take you to lunch." He eyed what was left of our snowballs. "If you're still hungry."

"Lunch? Me?" Rosemary looked like someone had just whacked her in the face with a board.

He smiled at her. "You." Then he turned to me. "You must be Glory."

"Yes, sir."

"So this has to be the famous Gus." He folded over to examine Gus's many wrinkles before obviously deciding he was deserving of a thorough ear scratching.

"Glory, you're invited to lunch too," he told me.

"I can't," I lied. "I promised my Papaw Jack I'd help him in the garden this afternoon." I was not going to barge in on Rosemary's time with her dad. She looked both excited and confused at the idea of lunch with him.

"Well, at least let me give you a ride home."

"Oh, we can walk," I said.

"It's pretty hot out. I don't mind."

"Well, um, Gus only rides in back seats. Not truck beds."

Rosemary's dad laughed. It sounded a lot like Rosemary's cackle the very first day I met her. "Gus is welcome to ride in the back seat."

I wasn't sure he quite understood the scope of Gus, despite Gus standing right in front of him. "Are you sure?"

"There is no way Gus can do anything to that back seat that hasn't already been done by one of my children. I promise," he said at the skeptical look on my face.

"Then yes, thank you. I think Gus would very much appreciate a ride home." Gus's tongue was hanging out of the side of his mouth, and I was pretty sure he wanted some air-conditioning just as badly as I did.

Once again, I had to boost Gus's behind into the truck. Rosemary's dad also found this very funny. He seemed to smile and laugh a lot. Maybe with five children you had to have a very good sense of humor.

"So, you're staying the whole summer with your grandparents?" he asked as he pulled onto the road.

But his phone rang before I could answer. Rosemary rolled her eyes.

"Allen Hymel. Yep. Hey, Mark. What can I do for you?"

Rosemary's dad spoke sentences that were in another language for all that I could understand. His job sounded like it had a lot of numbers.

"He gets so many work calls," Rosemary grumbled.

Gus leaned forward and sniffed Mr. Hymel's ear. Mr. Hymel leaned forward to escape the unwanted attention. He caught Rosemary's eye in the rearview mirror. "Mark? Can I call you back later? Great." He hung up. "I'm putting it on silent now. No lakes necessary." He fumbled with his phone before putting it down. "Now, what were we talking about?" His truck veered gently to the left, crossing the centerline.

"Dad," Rosemary said, her voice much calmer than mine would have been. "You're supposed to be driving."

"Oops." He steered the truck back into his lane. Luckily no one had been coming in the opposite direction.

"Dad loses things," Rosemary said. "Keys, kids, trains of thought."

"I've never misplaced a kid," he protested.

"That's because he used to make us wear leashes."

"They were not leashes. They were child harnesses."

Rosemary looked over at me. "Leashes."

"Fine. But five kids is a lot! Help me out here, Glory. They're always ganging up on me."

"Well, Gus doesn't seem to mind his leash all that much," I said.

"See?" Rosemary's dad pulled up in front of Nana Pat's house.

"Thanks for the ride," I said. I held tight to Gus's leash and opened the truck door.

"Any time," Mr. Hymel said.

"Guess you were right," Rosemary whispered as I climbed out of the truck. "We should all be more vocal like Gus."

Gus was exhausted when we got home. He sprawled out in the den and immediately fell asleep. Papaw Jack and I worked on the puzzle while I told him all about Gus's tracking session.

"He did much better today."

"He's an amazing dog," Papaw Jack said.

It started raining then, a soft patter on the roof that couldn't drown out Gus's snores. The den was lit by only two lamps, making it snug and cozy.

"The garden is happy." Papaw Jack snapped another piece into the puzzle. He was using his right hand a little more these days. "The weeds will be too." But I thought maybe the weeds were a good thing, not that I would tell him that. He and Nana Pat waged war against weeds. But Papaw Jack seemed stronger than when I'd first arrived, and I thought he had all those weeds to thank.

He definitely smiled more. But I knew that was because of Gus.

We'd made a good bit of progress on the puzzle by the time Nana Pat came home from the grocery store. Papaw Jack and I made an excellent team. He could see patterns in the shapes before I could, and I was better at seeing the subtle shades of color than he was.

Nana Pat poked her head in the den. She wasn't smiling. "Y'all come help with dinner."

We all three followed her into the kitchen.

"I wasn't talking to you," she told Gus.

But Gus didn't care. He invited himself places.

The rain had eased until it was more of a drizzle, a soft, blowing mist that looked like a shower curtain had dropped over the backyard.

"I'm craving BLTs," Nana Pat said as she took the bacon out of the fridge. "They're my favorite thing about summer."

Papaw Jack took the tomatoes and lettuce to the sink and washed them before handing them to me.

Gus practically sat on my foot while I tore the lettuce. He pawed my leg.

"Dogs don't eat lettuce," I told him.

He pawed my leg again, letting me know I had no idea what I was talking about.

"Fine," I whispered. Nana Pat was busy with the bacon. I snuck Gus a piece of lettuce.

He promptly tattled on me by chomping it as loudly as he could.

Papaw Jack snorted. "Must be part rabbit."

He certainly had the long ears.

Gus waddled over to where Nana Pat was taking the bacon out of the microwave. "Bacon is too expensive for dogs," she said without looking at him. She began assembling the sandwiches.

I filled three glasses with ice and tossed Gus a piece. He didn't catch it, but picked it off the floor and, upon realizing it wasn't the bacon he'd been waiting for, promptly spit it at me.

Papaw Jack chortled. I hurried and grabbed it before Nana Pat could notice. Her stony face made it quite clear that she hadn't forgiven me for yelling at her. I didn't need her mad at Gus too. "Spoiled brat," I told Gus under my breath. I tossed his ice in the sink and took the glasses to the table.

We sat down to eat.

Like Gus, I loved bacon—but the lettuce and tomato parts were not my favorite. I started to lift the bread off and remove the tomato, but Nana Pat shot me a glance. "Don't you dare. We are having BLTs for dinner."

It was the most she'd said to me since yesterday. I didn't argue. I needed to be allowed to stay. I dropped the bread back down and picked up the sandwich, steeling myself for the bite of mushy tomato.

Huh. I chewed. Nana Pat and Papaw Jack both watched me. It was really good.

"I didn't think I liked tomatoes," I said.

Nana Pat looked smug. "That's because you've never had any of my homegrown tomatoes. The ones you get at the store are junk. But in-season, real tomatoes? There's nothing like them."

I took another bite. She was right. She had put salt and pepper on the tomato, and the lettuce and bacon were both crisp, and it tasted a little like a summer sandwich, if summer had a taste. Papaw Jack was already halfway through his.

"Fried green tomatoes," Papaw Jack said.

"Yep," agreed Nana Pat. She looked at me. "I bet you've never had a fried green tomato either."

"No."

She looked very disappointed in me. But at least she was talking to me again. Her silence had been almost more than I could handle.

"They're a summer food—you can't buy green tomatoes at the store. It's one of the main reasons I keep growing tomatoes every summer."

A green tomato didn't sound very good to me, then again, neither did green eggs and ham, and that dude in the book ended up liking them just fine. That was the one rule in Nana Pat's house—I wasn't allowed to say I didn't like something until I'd tried it. She wouldn't make me eat something I hated, but to be honest, I hadn't once hated something she'd given me. So I would try fried green tomatoes too, even if I wasn't sure about them.

And if I didn't like them? I'd feed them to Gus when Nana Pat wasn't looking. Gus never said no to food.

I finished my sandwich. Nana Pat pointed to the plate in the center of the table. "Have another one. I made plenty."

We all ate another. Gus whined only once, but when Nana Pat gave him a dirty look, he lay down next to me. He'd learned fast what happened to dogs who begged—they got locked out.

I helped Nana Pat clear the table.

"Bacon is too expensive to give to dogs," she said again, and by the frown on her face, I was certain I was in trouble. I was about to protest that I hadn't given him any, despite feeling horrible about how sad he looked, but she continued before I could say anything. "But I soaked a piece of bread in the grease and left it over there for Gus. You can give it to him."

Even Nana Pat had fallen in love with Gus, though she did look a little horrified at herself for having been that sweet to something that made her house so dirty. Maybe she was going to let us stay after all.

"Sit," I told Gus. He obediently dropped into a sit. His

mouth started to water, dripping once, twice, on Nana Pat's clean floor. "Good boy," I said, quickly giving him the bread. "That's from Nana Pat," I told him. "You should say thank you."

He burped.

"Close enough." I giggled.

Nana Pat rolled her eyes, but I was pretty certain she had almost smiled. I hurriedly cleaned up the drool before she noticed.

Nana Pat gave Papaw Jack a look, and my skin went clammy. As a detective, I collected looks, and this one was ominous.

She *was* sending me away. She'd been nice because she was about to order me upstairs to pack.

"Why don't you sit down?" she said. "I want to talk to you."

I dropped hard into my chair. What would happen to Gus if I wasn't here? My skin felt prickly and hot, like I'd grabbed an electric fence.

"I went to see Mr. Babin today," she said. After the surgery he'd been moved to a rehabilitation room and was getting his strength back.

That was not what I'd expected her to say. But the fact that she hadn't immediately sent me to pack didn't make me feel any better. I didn't like how this conversation was starting. "How is he doing?"

"Much better." Nana Pat's face did not match her words. We should have been happy that Mr. Babin was healing. But none of us looked happy. All of our faces were drooping like Gus's. "They're sending Mr. Babin home on Monday."

Monday. I looked at Gus, who was sitting right by my knee hoping I had another piece of bacon-flavored bread. Gus was going home on Monday.

And I would lose my best friend.

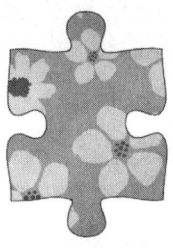

CHAPTER FIFTEEN

I spent that night in a nest of blankets next to Gus's bed. I couldn't imagine this room without him in it—his snores, his drool, his nosing his way into everything. I always knew I was going to have to give him back, but I was so happy having him here that I didn't really stop to think about how hard it was going to be to let him go.

I slept better now that he was here. I didn't have as many nightmares. And the possibility that Mom would come back for me seemed even more real when I looked at Gus. I'd never had a dog before, much less trained one, so he helped me to believe that anything was possible.

Gus woke me the next morning by sniffing my ear, his tail beating against the floor once he realized I was awake. Gus was the best alarm clock.

Nana Pat was already at work by the time Gus and I made it downstairs. Papaw Jack was pulling weeds in the garden. I let Gus out and stood at the window, watching him. He ran to Papaw Jack for morning pets. He sniffed the entire perimeter to make sure no intruders had breached the fence. He marched around the shed and startled a mockingbird.

Finally, he sat down in the yard and watched the morning. He sat so still that a butterfly landed on his back. It rested there awhile before flying away. Gus watched it until it disappeared over the fence.

I couldn't believe Mrs. Gill had ever thought Gus would have hurt Judy. He was the kindest, gentlest dog.

I loved him. I was going to miss him so much.

The sob was just sitting in my chest, but I refused to let it stand up. If I started crying now, I was afraid I wouldn't stop. And I wasn't going to spend my last couple of days with Gus crying.

"Beating the heat," Papaw Jack said when I joined him in the garden. I helped pull weeds. Gus dug a hole at the end of a row.

"What a good helper," I told him as I hurriedly replanted a squash plant he'd dug up. He stomped through the soft dirt and stuck his head in Papaw Jack's weed bucket and scared off a squirrel.

"Good boy," Papaw Jack said. "They're stealing tomatoes."

So, it wasn't Edna Gill after all.

"Do you think Gus will remember me?" I tossed a weed into the bucket.

Papaw Jack spoke even slower than usual, making sure I understood every word. "Of course he will. He loves you. He'll remember."

"Maybe Mr. Babin will still let me take him for walks some."

"I don't see why he wouldn't."

But what about when Mom came home? Gus wasn't going

to be the only one I would miss at the end of the summer. I hoped Mom wasn't so far away that we couldn't come back to visit.

"Will you miss me?" I asked Papaw Jack.

Papaw Jack stopped weeding. He rested his hands on his knees. "Are you going somewhere?"

That depended on Nana Pat. It was starting to look like she was going to let me stay after all. At least for now. "When I go home at the end of the summer." I just wished I knew where home was going to be.

Papaw Jack looked really sad then, and I regretted even bringing it up. "I'll miss you every day."

I wanted to believe him, but words could be shaped into lies much easier than actions could. And the fact was, before this summer, I hadn't seen him in over a year. "Maybe I could come back and visit."

"You better."

But I had no idea where Mom and I were going to be.

The day got hot fast. We went in and washed up. Gus sprawled out in the den while we worked on the puzzle for a while. We were almost done. We didn't talk again about me or Gus leaving.

Papaw Jack took his nap after lunch. Gus took one with him. I was sneaking a cookie while Gus wasn't looking when I saw the mail truck drive by. I tiptoed outside to get the mail. I hadn't done a very good job of being quiet because Gus was awake and waiting by the door when I came back in. He smelled the cookie on me. He gave me a look of supreme betrayal.

"Can't get anything past you," I said, rubbing the top of his head. I went to put the mail on the table in the hall when I saw the postcard in the middle of the stack. "Let's see where Dad has been," I told Gus. But the postcard wasn't from a specific town with a funny name. It was a generic postcard from Kentucky. I flipped it over.

I'm sorry.

My heart pounded. The postcard wasn't signed, but I recognized the handwriting. It was from my mom!

Nana Pat and Papaw Jack's address was scrawled across the right side, taking up twice as much room as the message. It didn't say who it was for. If she had signed it *Mom*, I would know it was for me. But she hadn't even done that.

Maybe the postcard was for Nana Pat and Papaw Jack. Was she sorry she hadn't come to visit them? Was she sorry they got stuck with me?

If the postcard was for me, was she sorry she left in the first place? Or was she sorry that she wasn't coming back?

I ran upstairs. Gus followed. I shut my bedroom door and threw the postcard on the bed. I didn't want to look at it. I wanted to examine every square inch to see if I'd missed something.

But I hadn't missed anything.

Two words.

I'd been waiting months to hear from her. And this was all I got.

It wasn't fair.

I glared at the picture of me and Mom. What a lie. I marched across the room and took it off the bulletin board. I tossed it in the drawer of my nightstand. I couldn't stand to look at it. My clue notebook sat on top of my nightstand. I knocked the notebook to the floor. Gus lumbered over and smelled it before looking at me like *What did you do that for?*

Because it was a lie too. All those notes, all those clues that I thought led up to the solution that Mom was coming home. She wasn't. And I wasn't going to care. If she didn't, then I didn't.

Only I did. I cared so much it hurt. I sank down to the floor and buried my face in Gus's neck. He sniffed my hair and then sat still, letting me hug him.

How could she just walk away and not come back? I could maybe understand her getting overwhelmed—no job, no apartment, no money—and wanting to start over again. But without me? Didn't she miss me? Love me?

She'd taken her favorite coffee mug, but she'd left me behind.

At the very least, she should have had the guts to tell me goodbye.

Gus licked the tears off my face. "Thanks, boy."

My phone rang. And even though Mom's phone had been disconnected for months, even though *I'm sorry* clearly meant *I don't want you*, I glanced at the screen with hope, just like I did every single time I got a call or text. I thought, again, that maybe this time it was Mom.

It wasn't. It was Dad.

And I answered, because even though I didn't want to talk to anyone right then, I was going to demand answers. He owed me that. They all did.

"Glory Bee! How's it going?" he asked.

"Fine." I could also lie.

"How's Gus?"

I was surprised he remembered Gus's name. He had a tendency to forget most of what I told him. "Fine."

"Just fine?"

"Gus has to go home," I said.

"That's good, right?"

What about that would he think was good? Gus was leaving me. Just like everyone else.

"That means his owner is better?" Dad asked when I didn't answer.

"Yes."

"You knew this was only temporary."

That wasn't the point. I had learned early on that most things in life were temporary. That didn't mean we weren't sad when they went away.

Why couldn't I just have one permanent thing in my life, one thing that stayed put? Stayed with me?

"Everything is going to be okay," he said.

"You're not listening to me!" He never did. He heard the words but he was always somewhere else.

Dad was silent for a second. I'd never yelled at him before. "I am listening. Gus is going home."

I needed him to hear what I wasn't saying. I needed him to understand what I was feeling and make me feel better. Wasn't that a parent's job? Maybe I needed to be more like Gus. He let everyone in the neighborhood know what he was feeling.

"I'm just tired of everyone leaving me," I finally admitted.

"Oh." Dad cleared his throat. "I'm sorry about that. You're right." He sounded like he wanted to be doing anything but having this conversation with me. "Well, then I have some good news."

I sat up. "You heard from Mom?"

"Well, no, I haven't heard anything from your mother. But I'm headed back to Louisiana. I'm going to be off for two weeks before I have to head back out."

"Two weeks?" He was going to be home for only two weeks? And then what?

"Come up with some things you want to do. Anything at all." He sounded excited. He'd missed my tone completely.

He didn't want to be a parent. Mom didn't want to be a parent. What did that leave me with?

"Why did you and Mom get married?" I'd never asked either one of them that before. But I was so tired of not knowing things.

His truck rumbled in the background. "Well," he finally said, his voice a little puzzled, "we fell in love."

"I'm going to need more than that." *Love* was a word you used. But it didn't really mean anything. Mom had told me she loved me before, but then she just left, no goodbye, no nothing.

Love was showing up. Love was standing next to someone when they were scared or imperfect.

Love meant staying.

"Your mom and I wanted the same thing when we met—to see the world. She was in college at LSU. She had a flat tire on the side of the road, and I stopped to help her fix it. We went to get coffee and ended up talking for hours about all the places we wanted to see."

A flat tire did not sound romantic.

"Over your mom's spring break, we packed up my truck and went on a road trip to Vegas. We came back married."

"And then what happened?"

"Well, the world turned out to be expensive. So we had to postpone seeing it. And then you came along."

I knew he didn't mean it to sound the way it did, but it felt like blame, like it was my fault life hadn't turned out the way they wanted.

Like that was an excuse for never being there.

"We were young," Dad said. "And you shouldn't marry someone just because you both want to travel."

"And kids? Did you even want those?"

"What?"

"Neither one of you wants me."

Gus stuck his nose in my face. Well, at least someone wanted me. But I didn't get to keep him forever.

"That's not true," Dad said.

"You spend all your time somewhere else. And Mom left and she isn't coming back."

The words sounded way worse out loud. The bottom dropped out of my stomach, like I'd missed a step on the staircase.

"You don't know that."

"Of course I do." My anger made me louder. "And so do you. You lied to me. You knew Mom wasn't on vacation.

You knew she wasn't coming back. You knew she'd left me for good and you let me believe she hadn't!"

"Glory, I don't know anything about your mom, what she will or won't do. Layla has always been a complete mystery to me."

"No. She sent you a text that said 'Your turn.' You knew she wasn't coming back the day you came to the apartment."

His voice was sharp. "How do you know that?"

"I looked at your phone."

I expected him to yell at me, but he didn't. He couldn't even care enough to get mad. He just sighed, a sound that seemed to contain all his disappointment. "I wish you hadn't done that."

Well, I wished a lot of things. "Why can't I know the truth?"

"That text could have meant it was my turn for a week. A month. Glory, what happened? Have you heard from her?"

I didn't answer right away. I didn't want to tell him. I wanted him to be just as clueless as I'd been. But then I realized the real reason I didn't want to tell him was because I was embarrassed. My mom left me. What did that say about me?

"She sent a postcard," I finally said, my voice flat. "It said 'I'm sorry.'"

"And?"

"That's it."

"Oh." And then he didn't say anything else. At all. Because Dad never dealt with the hard stuff.

Right then, I understood why Mom had gotten so mad

every time one of Dad's postcards had arrived. It was easy to slip a one-dollar piece of paper in the mail every once in a while. It was a lot harder to show up every single day.

My phone beeped. I glanced at the screen. It was Rosemary. "Dad, I've got to go."

"Wait."

I didn't wait. I hung up on him and answered Rosemary's call. "Hey."

"Glory?" I knew immediately that something was wrong. She sounded frantic. "Are you and Gus able to come over? Now?"

"What's happened?" I asked.

"Sebastian is missing."

CHAPTER SIXTEEN

"I'm on my way." I tossed my phone on the bed and hurried downstairs. Gus's leash was hanging by the back door. I didn't bother waking Papaw Jack up from his nap. There wasn't time. I snapped on Gus's leash and hurried out of the house.

Gus and I cut through the park, which was empty as usual. Rosemary met us at her back gate, frantic, her face red and sweaty. "Gus has to find him," she said.

This was the moment Gus and I had been training for. He'd found kittens already. He'd spent all summer finding Papaw Jack and Rosemary and Lydie and Sebastian. But those were all just practice. Now he had to find Sebastian when it mattered.

"Tell me what happened," I said.

"We were in the backyard," she said, pointing to Lydie, who was uncharacteristically quiet. "And then he was just gone."

"Are you sure he's not in the house?"

Rosemary scowled at me. "Do you think I would be this panicked? We've checked the house. He's not there."

"Okay. We need to hurry."

Rosemary glared at me, as if to say she'd been hurrying since way before I caught on. I ignored the glare. "The fresher the trail, the better. How long has he been gone?"

"Not sure. I've been looking for him for at least thirty minutes. I don't know how long before that he left."

If they'd been looking for thirty minutes, it meant they'd probably stomped all over the trail. That would make things a lot harder for Gus.

Jason rounded the corner of the house. "I walked all the way to the end of the cul-de-sac. I didn't see him."

"What about Allie?" I asked.

"She's at a friend's," Rosemary answered.

"If Allie were here, she would have already called out the National Guard," added Jason.

"She's even worse than our parents," Rosemary said.

"Do your parents know?"

She looked terrified and close to tears. "Not yet. I don't want to panic them."

Rosemary looked panicked enough all by herself.

"Brat is probably hiding nearby and laughing at all of us." Jason looked thoroughly grumpy about the whole situation. But his eyes darted down the street, and his fingers tapped his leg, which made me think he was trying to hide his worry.

"Don't call him a brat," Rosemary said. "He's little. And you were supposed to be in charge."

"This is not my fault. You know I sleep after football practice."

"You wouldn't be so sleepy if you didn't stay up all night!"

Jason made a face. "You sound like Mom. Maybe you should have been watching him. You don't have anything else to do anyway."

"Okay," I said, interrupting before Rosemary could attack Jason. She looked awful close to it. "I need everyone to go up on the porch so you'll stop stomping over the trail." I sounded a little like Nana Pat then—bossy and in charge. The best part was, they actually did it. "I also need something of Sebastian's, something that smells like him so Gus will know who he's looking for. Baby Frab?"

Rosemary disappeared into the house and returned with a grubby blanket. "He must have Baby Frab with him. This is his lovey. Can't sleep without it."

"Perfect." I took the blanket and held it up to Gus's nose. "Find it." I heard his nose working. "Find Sebastian."

Gus immediately put his nose to the ground and started sniffing. He pulled me toward the far side of the yard. A row of thick bushes grew against the weathered fence. He left the bushes and went back toward the porch. If Sebastian had been playing here, he'd probably run all over this yard, not just today, but the day before that and the day before that. His scent had to be everywhere—I wasn't sure how Gus was going to know which one to follow.

"It's fine," I said at Rosemary's worried expression. "Give him a minute." Gus had to catalog all of those scents in his brain. That took time.

He pulled me toward the park. He was trotting now,

and it took all my strength to hold on to him and not get dragged down.

Lydie and Jason stayed on the porch, but Rosemary followed. "We've got this," I promised her. I would not let anyone else in my life disappear.

"I'll stay back," Rosemary said, but I heard the steel in her voice. She was not going to stay home.

"Stay well back," I told her. "Sometimes he needs to backtrack and I don't want you to contaminate anything."

Twice I stopped and had Gus sniff the blanket to remind him of who we were looking for. He'd pulled me right through the center of the park, but now he was walking slower, meandering back and forth. When he stopped to watch a squirrel dart across his path, then looked up at me with his tongue hanging out of the side of his mouth, I knew he had lost the trail.

My heart sank. We hadn't yet practiced with cross scents. There were at least hundreds of other smells out here—how was he supposed to know how to find Sebastian's?

Because of the blanket. Because we had practiced this. I knew he could do this.

"Find it," I told Gus as I let him sniff the blanket. I felt a lump forming in my throat. "Please," I whispered. "It's Sebastian. We have to find him."

Because this wasn't hide-and-seek. This wasn't some game we were playing. This was real. Something really bad could happen to Sebastian if we didn't find him soon.

"What?" Rosemary asked as she came closer.

"He's just regrouping," I said. I scanned the park. Was Sebastian here and didn't know we were looking for him?

Rosemary narrowed her eyes. "Gus can't do this, can he?"

"Yes he can!" My heart pounded in my chest, and my stomach felt like I'd just eaten a fistful of snakes. "He's not giving up. Gus won't quit until he finds Sebastian. I won't either." I was not abandoning Sebastian. I was not leaving him alone wherever he was. "Let's go back to the beginning."

Shame settled on my shoulders like a heavy blanket as we stepped back into Rosemary's yard without Sebastian. Only Lydie was still outside.

"Lydie, did you see where Sebastian went?" I asked.

"No." She looked very close to tears.

"Were y'all playing hide-and-seek?"

Lydie shook her head, her curly hair bouncing. "We were playing pirates. And he said he knew where there was a buried treasure, and I said no he did not, and he said he did too." She started to cry. "But I know there isn't really a buried treasure and he isn't going to make me walk the plank."

"Okay, Lydie, it's okay." Rosemary patted her sister's shoulder. "Go inside with Jason."

And Lydie, who almost never did what her sister told her to do, went inside.

"Okay, where should we start?" I had to start thinking like a detective. "Where might he have gone?"

"If I knew that, I would have tried it already," she snapped.

"Has he ever wandered off before?"

"Not like this. He was supposed to be in the backyard

the day you and Gus met him in the park. And he got away from Mom one time in the grocery store, but he just went to the candy aisle."

We'd already checked the park. "Would he have gone looking for candy now? Walked to the store?"

"He doesn't have any money. He might be little, but he knows how money works."

Gus tugged me back toward the bushes against the fence. He disappeared into the thick leaves.

I repeated everything Lydie had told us inside my head. Pirates. Planks. "Is there a buried treasure somewhere?" I asked.

Rosemary rolled her eyes. "In Sweet Olive?" Then she gasped. "Somewhere near the school! Sebastian came home one day talking about how his teacher had taken them on a nature walk and he'd found buried treasure. He had a rock that had something shiny running through it. I mostly just ignored him, but Dad acted all interested and it took up most of the dinner conversation. I remember because I'd gotten an A on my math test and didn't even get to talk about it. And I'd studied really hard for it too."

"Let's start there." I gave Gus's leash a little tug. "Gus. Come on."

He was not coming out of the bushes. I squatted down and peered inside.

Gus's behind wiggled as he tried to force himself through a hole in the fence. "Good boy!" I stood up. "I think Sebastian went through here."

We went to the other side of the fence and I reminded Gus

who we were looking for by letting him smell the blanket again. Gus tugged me down a narrow strip of grass that ran along the neighborhood backyards. Fences lined some sides, and trees hung over, providing us with a shady canopy.

"Allie and Jason and I used to play here all the time when we were little," Rosemary said. "We pretended we had a fort just there." She pointed to the weeping willow that hung over the grass. It was a cool place to climb inside and hide.

I heard voices coming from behind the curtain of leaves. Gus stuck in his head.

"Ah!"

Two boys emerged into the sunlight. Not Sebastian—Tate and Scotty.

Rosemary marched right up to them and scowled. "Where is my little brother?"

Both of them kept an eye on Gus, who was sniffing at a random clump of grass. "We saw him run off that way," one of the boys said, pointing left.

"Because y'all were bullying him?" Rosemary snarled.

"We didn't even talk to him," the other boy said. "Swear."

"He just ran by. Looked like he knew where he was headed."

"Thanks," I said. Rosemary still looked mad. But at least we knew we were going in the right direction. "If you see him, tell him to go home."

Rosemary narrowed her eyes. "Nicely."

Both boys nodded.

We didn't have time to waste. I tugged at Gus's leash and got us moving toward the school again.

Every once in a while, Gus would drop his head and sniff, but mostly he just seemed happy to have been invited along on the adventure. I'd never seen any of the schools in Sweet Olive. Rosemary told me that the high school was on the other side of town but the elementary was tucked down in the center of a neighborhood.

Hardly anyone was outside in their backyards as we passed. Most of the adults would be at work, and the kids were inside with the air conditioners. Rosemary and I were both sweating, and Gus's tongue was hanging out. He would need some water soon. We all would.

Which made me wonder about Sebastian. I hoped we were right and he was just digging for buried treasure somewhere. I didn't want to think about him hurt.

So I didn't think about that at all. I focused on our destination.

The grassy alleyway led us onto a sidewalk, and I could just see the red roof of the school a couple of streets over.

"This was a long walk for him to do by himself," I said. We'd been walking for probably forty-five minutes by then.

Rosemary looked both angry and scared. "I know. I hope he's okay, because I'm going to let him have it. He knows better." She shook her head. "I absolutely expect this of Lydie. Jason. Even Allie is stubborn, though she is a rule follower. But Sebastian is the good one."

We waited for a car to pass before crossing the street. The school was empty and silent, which was a little eerie. Schools were usually bustling, parking lots full of cars, playgrounds full of loud kids.

I stopped just outside the padlocked gate of the fence that surrounded the whole school. "Now what?"

Rosemary cupped her hands to her mouth. "Sebastian!" she shouted.

We all three listened closely. I held my breath and strained my ears but still heard nothing.

"Where was this nature walk?" I asked.

"No idea. But it had to be near here, because he said they did it at recess."

The school sat alone on its lot, surrounded by a fence and bordered on three sides by roads. Across the road on two sides were houses. Trees lined the third side. I could just see the highway peeking through. The back was edged by thicker trees.

"I think that's our best bet," I said, pointing to the line of trees behind the school.

We had to walk the long way around because of the fence. The temperature dropped at least a couple of degrees as we stepped into the shade of the trees. The woods weren't too thick; sunlight filtered down in places. There wasn't a path or anything running through here, just leaves and undergrowth.

"Sebastian!" we both called. No answer.

I let Gus smell the blanket again. But he sat down and looked up at me, panting.

"Jason was right." Rosemary's voice was thick. "I should have been watching even if it was Jason's turn."

"You can't put all that responsibility on yourself. You aren't the only one in charge of Sebastian." I squeezed her hand. "We're going to find him."

She looked down at Gus in doubt.

I didn't have Gus's nose, but I did have the mind of a detective. I scanned the ground. There had to be clues.

I saw only leaves and shadows.

"Do you remember anything else he said about the treasure?"

Rosemary thought. "He was talking about trolls, which didn't make sense." She chewed on her bottom lip. "And goats? That can't be right."

Goats. Trolls. That snagged on something at the back of my mind. "Is there a bridge around here somewhere?"

"A bridge?"

"Yeah, a troll bridge," I said. "Like in that story with the goats and the troll."

"Oh yeah! But I have no idea about a bridge."

"Okay." I wasn't giving up hope. We'd just have to find it. I gave a light tug on the leash. "Come on, buddy. I know you're tired. But we can't quit yet."

We'd been walking for about five minutes when I saw the trickle of water. "Look!" A shallow ditch ran along in front of us. "If a bridge goes over it, it has to be that way." I pointed left. "Because the other way is the school."

"Are you sure?" Rosemary asked.

"No. But it's worth a shot."

We kept walking. We shouted for Sebastian. But the only answer came from a couple of squirrels.

Gus suddenly tugged on my arm, pulling away from the ditch, away from where the bridge would be. I tugged back. Gus didn't turn around. I had to stop.

"What's wrong?" Rosemary asked.

"Gus wants to go that way."

"There wouldn't be a bridge that way."

"I know."

"Gus can't find him," Rosemary said. "We stick to the plan."

I looked into Gus's face. His wrinkles made him look serious and sad. We'd spent enough time together that I was fairly certain of what he was trying to tell me. And this time, I was going to listen.

"Are you sure?" I asked him.

He sniffed the ground and pulled at his leash. I had to trust him. Gus had always shown up for me.

I followed him.

"Glory!" Rosemary shouted.

But Gus was pulling harder now. I was almost running to keep up with him, and my feet tripped and snagged over fallen branches and exposed tree roots. We left Rosemary behind as Gus dragged me over to something red lying on the ground. My heart began pounding in my chest as we got closer. "Baby Frab!" I shouted back to Rosemary.

I let Gus thoroughly sniff the red stuffed animal lying on the ground. "Find it," I told him. "Find Sebastian, Gus."

"He's been here." Rosemary sounded relieved and surprised. But I wasn't surprised. Gus was the very best boy. Rosemary picked up the stuffed crab. Gus forged ahead, nose to the ground.

This time I was fairly certain Gus was on the trail. He never lifted his head, and Rosemary and I were both jogging to stay with him.

He zigged right and zagged left, but not in a way that made me believe he'd lost his way.

He was really doing this.

I saw Sebastian first. He was curled into a ball at the base of a tree. Gus gave a loud bark when he saw him, and he jerked the leash right out of my hand as he ran to Sebastian.

By the time I'd caught up, Gus was smothering Sebastian in kisses.

"Sebastian!" Rosemary cried. She sank to the ground and pulled him into a hug. "Are you hurt?"

"No." Sebastian blinked sleepily. "I just got lost, and I remembered what Mrs. Hansen told us about that—to stay calm and stay put." He wiped his face. "I stayed put. But not so calm. I cried myself to sleep." He looked embarrassed.

"You were very smart," I told him. "And very brave."

"And Gus found me," he said, smiling for the first time and patting my dog.

Mostly. But Rosemary and I let Gus take the credit.

"Don't you ever wander off again!" She handed him Baby Frab.

Sebastian hugged the stuffed animal tight to his chest. His face was streaked with tears and dirt. "I'm sorry," he said. "I wanted to prove to Lydie I could find the buried treasure."

"Good boy," I told Gus, making sure he knew he had done exactly right. I scratched his ears and patted his side. "You are a very good boy." He was going to get so many treats.

"It's getting late," Rosemary said. It was still daylight, but that was because the sun didn't set until after 8 p.m.

Sebastian had been gone for nearly two hours by now. "We'd better get home and let everyone know you're okay."

Home. The word was painful instead of comforting. Now that the emergency was over and the adrenaline had worn off, the rest of the day came rushing in. Rosemary and Sebastian knew exactly where their home was. It wasn't going anywhere. And they had each other.

But my mom wasn't coming home. I let that truth settle over me. I'd been looking for that truth ever since Mom left, and now that I'd found it, I didn't really want it. It had been easier believing that Mom was coming home. This truth hurt.

Mom didn't want to be found. She didn't want me.

Rosemary and Sebastian held hands as they walked back toward the school. Gus and I fell behind.

I wanted to cry and scream. I wanted to curl into a ball at the base of a tree like Sebastian had.

I wanted so many things to be different.

But I kept moving forward. Gus still needed me to get him home safely. I held tight to his leash and followed him toward Rosemary's.

Mom left. Dad was going to keep leaving. Gus was going home.

And I would be alone.

CHAPTER SEVENTEEN

We were halfway back to Rosemary's house when a cop pulled up beside us and rolled down his window. "Are you Rosemary and Sebastian?"

We'd been gone long enough that Rosemary's parents must have called the police.

"Yes, sir," Rosemary answered. "And Glory."

"I found them," the cop said into his radio. He turned to us again. "Y'all better hop in the back."

"Are we getting arrested?" Sebastian asked. He looked close to crying again. He'd had a very bad day.

"Of course not. I just need to get you home safe."

"Can I have your badge number?" I asked.

The cop's expression went blank for a minute, and then he smiled. "That's smart."

"She's going to be a detective," Rosemary said proudly.

I'd never had a friend who was so proud of me before.

"I'm Officer James Williams." He showed us his badge.

Rosemary and Sebastian both looked at me. "Seems legit," I said. They climbed in the back of the cop car.

"Gus too?" I asked, assuming he would not want my

slobbering dog in the back seat. We were both tired, but we could walk back if we had to.

"Him too," Officer Williams answered.

Gus didn't really want to go for a ride. I hoisted his behind up while Sebastian promised him treats. Gus seemed very put out when he finally got into the back seat and realized there were no treats. He did not understand the word *later*.

I realized how much trouble we were in when we pulled up in front of Rosemary's house. Her entire family was standing in the front yard, and another cop was parked in the driveway. Of course they were worried. Nobody had known where we were. I felt awful that it had taken so long to find Sebastian.

"Don't you ever do that to me again," Rosemary's mom said as soon as Rosemary and Sebastian had gotten out of the car. Gus and I stood off to the side as Rosemary's mom fell to her knees and threw her arms around them. The rest of the family surrounded them, and they were soon lost in the middle of a family hug.

"We were worried sick," their dad added. His hair was sticking up more than usual.

I knew Rosemary had her own problems with her family sometimes, but I hoped she appreciated how much they loved her. Rosemary always knew where home was, and she always had people waiting there for her.

She didn't get postcards that just said *I'm sorry*.

I blinked fast and squatted next to Gus. We had each other.

For now.

"Glory!"

I lifted my head. That was Nana Pat's voice.

And there she was, looking just as worried as Rosemary's mom. Papaw Jack was there too. And Aunt Kat! With Mervin! Nana Pat pulled me into a hug.

"Where in the world have you been?" she asked, but she didn't let me answer. "Your dad was frantic when he called us!"

"My dad?"

"He said you were upset with him. But you weren't in your room. And you weren't answering your phone."

I patted my pockets and realized I'd left my phone on my bed.

"You didn't come home." Nana Pat's hands were actually shaking. "We thought you'd run away."

"To where?" I asked. "I don't have anywhere else to go."

Nana Pat's eyes filled with tears.

"We were scared," Papaw Jack said. He squeezed my hand and patted Gus on the head.

"We aren't mad," Rosemary's dad told her.

"I'm mad," Rosemary's mom added, at the same time that Nana Pat harrumphed. "You call us, understand? Even if you're worried about getting in trouble. If anything bad ever happens, you call us immediately."

"Okay, we're a little mad," he amended. "But mostly we were just afraid."

"Let the girl breathe, Patty," Aunt Kat told Nana Pat, who still hadn't let me go. She stepped back but kept her hand on my arm, like she was afraid I might disappear again. "Let them talk."

And the story came out. Rosemary and I took turns, and by the end, Rosemary's parents had decided Gus and I were heroes.

"It was Gus, really," I said. He'd done most of the work.

"I owe you a hamburger, Gus," Rosemary's mom said, and she squatted down and loved on Gus a little bit. She looked up at me. "But promise me y'all will not go wandering off by yourselves again." I nodded. Then she stood up and pulled me into a hug. Rosemary's dad patted my arm. "We are so lucky to have you and Gus."

"I told you he was the smartest dog," Lydie said.

"And you were right," her mom told her.

Lydie flashed a confident smile. "I always am."

Nana Pat's phone rang. "Edna, we've got her. Yes, she's fine. Thank you so much for all your help. All right. I'll tell her."

"Edna Gill?" I asked when she'd hung up.

"Everyone has been worried sick," Nana Pat said. "When we went out looking, Edna volunteered to stay at our house in case you showed up."

I had a family. I had a family who had their arms around me and had been waiting at home for me and sent the police out looking for me.

I had people, more than one, watching out for me.

"We were hoping Mervin could do a little of what Gus does and sniff y'all out," Aunt Kat said. Mervin was leaning against Gus, who was tolerating the attention.

"I tried putting him on the trail like you do with Gus," Papaw Jack said.

Nana Pat got her two cents in. "But the only thing he found was a dead squirrel."

Aunt Kat rolled her eyes and looked at Mervin with nothing but love. "He's a work in progress."

Nana Pat smiled at me. "I think we all are. Oh!" She jumped a little and took out her phone again. "I better let your dad know you're okay."

I'd never had that many people caring for me before. I'd been staying home alone, walking down to the corner store by myself, getting myself up and ready for school, for so long. Mom trusted me to take care of myself, so I had. But I had to admit, it was nice being taken care of for a change. It was nice having people worry about me.

"Tim," Nana Pat said when my dad answered, "we've got her. She's fine. Yes. We will. Bye." Nana Pat hung up the phone.

He hadn't even wanted to talk to me. He must have been really mad.

Gus fell asleep with his head in my lap on the ride home and went right back to sleep as soon as we got inside. We were all exhausted. We ate cereal for dinner, too tired for anything else.

"Glory," Nana Pat said, her voice heavy as she carried her bowl to the sink, "we need to talk."

This was the moment. Where would I go if they didn't want me? "I'm sorry I didn't tell you where I was going. Please don't send me away."

Nana Pat looked up in surprise. "What?" She glanced at Papaw Jack, who was sitting next to me at the table, then back to me.

"I'm sorry I yelled at you and Aunt Kat. But I don't want to stay with strangers."

Nana Pat sat down across from me. She folded her hands together on top of the table. "You will not be staying with strangers, not while there is breath in my body. I would never send you away. What in the world gave you that idea?"

I dropped my head and stared at my lap. "You were mad at me."

"I'm not mad at anyone. I was worried."

"We all were," Papaw Jack added.

"Before tonight. After I yelled at Aunt Kat's."

Nana Pat's features softened. "You were upset about your mom. And had every right to be. I'm not mad."

"But you haven't been talking to me."

Nana Pat sighed. "I was giving you space. I think that's where I messed up with your mom. I didn't give her space when she needed it."

But I didn't want space. Mom was giving me way too much of it. Dad too.

"Well, it made me think you didn't want me anymore."

"Glory." I realized with horror that Nana Pat sounded like she was going to cry again. I wasn't sure I could handle more of her tears. "I'll always want you."

I looked at her. I was tired of everyone dodging the truth. I wanted all of it. "Then why didn't you try harder? Why didn't you try harder to see me for the past year?"

Papaw Jack's face was stony. Nana Pat looked like all the breath had been knocked clean out of her. I didn't think she was going to answer. But she finally did. "Because I was afraid."

I knew adults could get afraid, but it never ceased to surprise me. They were in charge. They were supposed to fix things so that we didn't have to be scared.

"Afraid of what?"

"That if I pushed, I would lose you and your mom forever."

And I realized then that Nana Pat missed my mom as much as I did.

"Your mom and I had a fight—a bad one. We'd always fought. We're too much alike—stubborn and independent. And I criticized her as a parent, and she told me to butt out and that if I didn't, I wouldn't ever see you or her again. So I butted out. And she let me talk to you on the phone."

"And that was enough?"

"Of course not! I was always hoping she'd forgive me."

"Did you ask her to?"

"Maybe not in those words."

Adult shortsightedness again. Bless their hearts. "Then maybe you should have used those words."

Papaw Jack's shoulders sagged as he listened. He was good at not interrupting. But right then I needed answers. I was mad at both of them.

"I know she isn't on vacation."

"Well, I don't know that," Nana Pat said. "Not for sure."

I gave her my best detective look. In books and movies, the detective can stare into suspects' souls and suddenly they're admitting to every bad deed. I'd been practicing in the mirror. I tried it on Nana Pat.

She stared right back. "I'm telling you everything I know."

I slumped in my chair. "I know." But only because I'd overheard her conversation with Aunt Kat. "But you'd be the first adult who did."

"I don't have any idea where she is. She could be on a vacation for all I know."

"She can't afford a vacation," I admitted. "And if you'd been there, if you'd apologized or tried harder to be in my life, then maybe she wouldn't have left at all. She needed help, and she was alone."

Papaw Jack spoke up. "What do you mean?"

"She got fired. She ran out of money. We got evicted. And she didn't think she could ask you for help!"

Nana Pat just wilted. There was no other word for it. She was sitting up tall, and then she sort of shrank, like a drooping flower that had been sitting out too long. She bowed her head and closed her eyes. She looked ten years older.

I wondered why Dad hadn't told her himself. Maybe he was ashamed too.

"We would have helped her," Nana Pat said.

And I knew they would have. But why didn't my mom ask? It was the question that had been bothering me the most. If she had just asked, maybe she wouldn't have had to leave me behind.

"Things would be a lot different if I understood your mother. I'm sure she'd say the same about me. And things would be different if we had talked. But we didn't. Your mom has had to carry a lot by herself," Nana Pat said.

"Not by herself." I sat up straighter in my chair. "I helped." But even as I said it, I knew I hadn't done enough. If I had, Mom wouldn't have left.

"I know you did. But you are a child. You should get to be a child, no matter what decisions the adults make in your life."

There was that word again—*should*.

"No, your dad should have done more too." She held up her hand when she saw I was going to defend him. "I like your dad. He's a decent man. But he should have been around more. Papaw Jack and me too. We should have all helped more, even when she said she didn't want us to." Nana Pat looked up at Papaw Jack. "Why didn't she come to us if it was that bad?"

He didn't answer.

But I did. "Maybe she didn't want to hear 'I told you so.'"

Nana Pat looked like she was about to tell me she never would have done that, but she stopped. Nana Pat would have helped—but she probably would have fussed too, and we all knew it.

"She's not coming back." I spoke softly, trying not to jostle all the broken pieces of me.

She wouldn't work on any more puzzles after I was asleep. Wouldn't watch true crime shows with me. Wouldn't bring me home leftovers from the restaurant or take me to Goodwill for books.

But she had stopped doing those things long before she'd left. I realized in that moment that I had watched my mom disappear little by little before she'd actually walked away.

Gus shoved his head in my lap. I ran my hand along the top of his head once, twice, three times. My breathing steadied.

"She's not coming back," I said again. Nana Pat and Papaw Jack needed that truth as much as I did. They loved her too.

"I really don't know what she'll do," Nana Pat said. "She is your mother, but she is also my baby girl, even if I'm so angry at her right now I could spit nails. I'm scared for her and mad at her and so very, very sad."

"Me too," I admitted. Anger and hurt filled up all the space inside me. In that moment, I couldn't imagine ever having room for anything else.

"And I'm mad at myself," Nana Pat admitted. "For so many things. The adults screwed this up. I'm sorry, Glory."

"But what about after the summer?" I asked. "I don't want to go to foster care."

"Why in the world would you think you would?" Nana Pat sounded angry.

"Dad isn't going to stick around. He told me today he would be home for two weeks before going back on the road." I gave a hollow laugh. "Two whole weeks."

Papaw Jack and Nana Pat looked at each other across the kitchen table. "He said you were upset after his call."

"You have a home here," Papaw Jack said. He spoke slow and deep and steady. "Forever, if that's what you want."

"Well, I'm sorry if I don't trust everything y'all tell me. You've disappeared before. Who says you won't disappear again?"

"We deserve that," Nana Pat said. "And I hope you'll keep letting us try to earn that trust back. That starts with honesty. I'm not very good at talking about the hard stuff. But I should have."

"Hard things take practice," I said.

"How did you get so smart?" she asked.

"My side of the family," Papaw Jack said.

Nana Pat narrowed her eyes. "I've met your side of the family," she reminded him.

"Maybe just me, then." Papaw Jack winked at me.

And Nana Pat didn't argue. She always did let Papaw Jack have the last word, even if it took him a while to get to it.

"Your mom loves you," Papaw Jack said. "That might be hard to see right now, but she does."

"She left without saying goodbye. That's not love."

"Love takes all shapes," he said.

"Maybe she wanted more for you than she could give," added Nana Pat.

Maybe believing all that made this easier on them. But I wouldn't live in a lie.

"Do you think Mom regretted me?" It was a question I'd been too terrified to even think, but it had been crouching in the shadows, and all of a sudden, it jumped right out of my mouth. "She wanted to see the world, and I was the reason she didn't get to."

"Nothing is your fault. Nothing. Do you hear me?" She didn't sound sad anymore. She was bossy Nana Pat again. She scowled at the uncertainty on my face. "It is not your fault that your mother didn't do everything she wanted to do. It is not your fault she left. And if she doesn't come back, well, that won't be your fault either. You are a gift."

It didn't feel that way.

"When Gus needed a place to stay, you gave him one," Papaw Jack said.

Nana Pat nodded. "He tracked in mud and made messes and you still wanted him."

"Of course I did! I love him!" I felt so lucky he got to be mine, at least for a little while.

"Exactly. Gus is a blessing to you, not a burden."

I didn't think I'd ever hear Nana Pat call Gus a blessing.

"And you are a blessing, not a burden. You remember that. And if I made you feel otherwise, I am so very sorry." She got up and hugged me. I hugged her back.

Gus, not wanting to be left out, gave each of us a very wet kiss.

Gus's first family had given him away. But that had said more about them than him.

And if that could be true for Gus, then it could be true for me too.

CHAPTER EIGHTEEN

I was still in bed the next morning when a huge rumble came from down the street. Gus barked at the noise, suddenly awake, and jumped to his feet.

"I'm up," I mumbled. I rubbed the sleep out of my eyes and opened my bedroom door. Gus barreled down the stairs, howling and baying. If Nana Pat and Papaw Jack weren't already up, they were now.

Gus was guarding the front door when I made it downstairs. "It's too early for all that," I told him. I peered out the window.

Dad was trying to park his rig. I was suddenly awake. "Dad's here!" I shouted in the small space between Gus's last bark and his next.

Nana Pat and Papaw Jack, still in their bathrobes, emerged from the kitchen, coffee mugs in hand.

What was Dad doing here?

I left Gus inside and went out to wait on the front porch.

Dad couldn't get his rig into the driveway, so he pulled as far out of the road as possible. He wasn't going to be able to keep that there for long. Dad opened his driver's side door and climbed out. He looked tired.

"Glory," Dad said.

I hopped off the porch and threw my arms around his waist. He held me for a minute, then stepped back and examined my face. "Are you okay?" he asked.

He could have just asked me that last night for himself. But he hadn't wanted to talk to me. "I'm fine."

"I needed to see for myself."

"Why now?" I couldn't keep the edge out of my voice.

He raked a hand down his face. "I'm going to need some coffee."

Once again, dodging the important questions.

Gus greeted us at the door in his usual dramatic way. He barked and bellowed and fussed at me for not letting him come with me. Dad stopped just inside the door.

"He's sweet," I said. "Just loud."

"No sneaking in," Papaw Jack said. He shook Dad's hand with his left. Dad looked a little uncomfortable. "Coffee?"

"Yes, please."

Dad looked even warier as he stepped into the kitchen. "Tim," Nana Pat said. "How was the drive?"

"Long." He looked like he'd driven all night.

"Cream and sugar?" Nana Pat asked.

"Black."

She handed him a large mug of coffee. "I bet you could use some breakfast."

"I wouldn't say no."

"I think we need to talk," I told Dad. Nana Pat and Papaw Jack and I had said a lot of truths last night. Now it was Dad's turn.

Papaw Jack put his hand on my shoulder. "It's easier to listen with a full belly. Coffee helps too."

I did not agree with his assessment of coffee, but if the adults needed it, I'd wait.

I didn't think I was hungry, but the minute I smelled bacon, my stomach rumbled. Gus's did too. I fed him while Nana Pat cooked breakfast.

Gus rested his head on my foot while we ate. Mostly I thought he was hoping I'd drop something. But I liked to think he was letting me know he was on my side.

Dad talked about his trip. Nana Pat talked about the garden and what we'd been up to this summer. Papaw Jack said very little, less than usual, and I wondered if it was because he'd gotten used to talking in front of me and wasn't yet used to it in front of Dad.

There was a lot of trust that needed to be earned around here.

For my part, I didn't talk at all, afraid that everything I'd been thinking and feeling would come rolling out and I wouldn't be able to stop it. We ate. We cleaned up the kitchen.

"Guess we'd better have that talk." Dad looked just as nervous as I felt.

"Let's go in the living room," Nana Pat said. "We better be comfortable if we're about to talk ourselves uncomfortable."

No more hiding from the hard stuff. No more pretending everything was okay. That hadn't gotten us anywhere good.

Gus plodded along behind us. He started to veer into the den, thinking this was like any other day and he was going to be curling up at Papaw Jack's feet, but he quickly corrected and followed us into the living room.

Papaw Jack and Dad sat on the sofa. Nana Pat took a poufy chair. I, however, was too antsy to sit down. My stomach churned and my skin felt itchy, like all my anger and worry had been rubbing up underneath for so long that it had chafed. Gus sat down in the doorway and watched all of us.

Maybe he felt that something was off.

Before I could say anything, Dad spoke up. "You are a twelve-year-old girl, and I want to make it clear that you do not get to go anywhere without permission."

This was where he wanted to start?

"It doesn't feel good, does it?" I asked. "Not knowing where people are."

Mom left without telling anyone anything. Dad took jobs without thinking about anyone else. So he didn't get to be mad when I did the same thing. It obviously ran in the family.

Except that I was there for those I cared about.

"I don't like your tone," Dad said.

"I'm sorry. But I don't like how I've been treated." I was going to be just like Gus—unafraid of making noise and taking up space. For once, Dad was going to listen to me—really listen.

"Mom's not coming back." It wasn't any easier to say now than it had been last night. It felt like pressing on a bruise. Maybe it always would. "She told you it was your turn to raise me and then you didn't want your turn either."

"That's not true," Dad said.

"Which part?" Nana Pat asked.

Dad rubbed the back of his neck and grimaced. "The last text Layla sent me said 'Your turn.'"

Nana Pat looked a little sick.

"But of course I wanted my turn," Dad told me. "I just had to go to work. Adults have responsibilities, Glory."

"They sure do. And I'm one of yours."

Dad hung his head. Papaw Jack gave me a small nod. And Nana Pat looked at me with pride.

"Gus needed me this summer, and I showed up." My voice shook. "I loved him and spent time with him and didn't make other plans or just leave him alone. You can't come home for two weeks and then leave again. Where am I supposed to live? What about school?"

"She was worried she'd have to go into foster care," Nana Pat told him. She sounded almost as angry as she had last night.

Dad looked like she'd punched him. "I guess I don't know how to be a full-time dad." He looked smaller somehow, sitting on Nana Pat's couch.

Nana Pat softened her voice. "You can learn."

"It's on-the-job training." Papaw Jack smiled.

"If you want to," I added, staring at the scuffed toes of my shoes.

"Want to? Glory, you're my daughter."

I looked at him then. "And now that means more than just weekends."

Dad flinched slightly.

Nana Pat spoke up. "We'll raise Glory. We'd be glad to. We failed her before. We aren't going to do that again."

"No one has done right by Glory," Papaw Jack said slowly, carefully. "And we are all going to do better. Because she deserves it."

All that anger and all that hurt was still there. But they shifted over just enough to make a little space for some joy. I smiled at Papaw Jack.

Dad turned to me. There was nothing laid-back about him in that moment. "I would like to try, if you'll let me."

He was letting me decide. I was finally getting a say in what happened to me.

I'd said a lot of truths the last couple of days. I must have run through all my words. Because I could only nod.

"Glory needs stability," Nana Pat said. "So you're either going to have to get a new job or you're going to have to move closer so we can help. We're family now. Glory makes us family."

"She's a little bossy," I said with an apologetic laugh. Nana Pat snorted. But I didn't want him to keep me from seeing Nana Pat and Papaw Jack like Mom had.

"A little bossy," Dad agreed with a tight smile. "But she's right. I'm man enough to admit I'll need help. I can rent a trailer here just as easily as I can in Lafayette. That way Glory could stay with you and me both."

And in that moment, what I felt was relief. I was going to get to keep Dad and Nana Pat and Papaw Jack.

※

Dad and I spent the day together. I showed him the puzzle Papaw Jack and I had almost finished. I told him about training Gus and how we'd found Sebastian. He wasn't too mad anymore. He listened.

He loved Gus immediately, like we all did. He howled and then laughed when Gus answered him. He told me more about the dog he'd had as a kid, how they'd gone fishing every day after school in the pond behind his house. He told me more stories in one afternoon than he had maybe ever.

It would take me a while to trust that he and Nana Pat and Papaw Jack weren't going to leave me. But I would try, because they were trying. It was a messy start, but it was a start.

"I have to get this trailer back," Dad said later in the afternoon. "And it looks like there's a lot to do. Do you want to ride with me?"

Dad had never once asked me to ride in his truck. "I can't," I told him. "I'm still responsible for Gus. At least until Monday."

He nodded. "Are you going to be okay?"

I would have to be. Gus wasn't mine. Though that didn't feel true at all. He was my very best friend. But he was going home.

"Spaghetti all right for dinner?" Nana Pat asked as we came downstairs.

"I'm not staying for dinner," Dad said. Nana Pat's eyebrows jumped into her hairline. Dad held up his hands. "Now that I know Glory is okay, I have to go drop this trailer off. I'm not running out on anyone."

Nana Pat relaxed a bit.

"But would it be all right if I stayed here for a little while longer?" I asked.

"I would like it more than anything else in this world," she said.

"Same." Papaw Jack's voice was strong and clear on that one word.

In the end, the people who left didn't matter as much as the people who stayed.

CHAPTER NINETEEN

Gus woke me up on Monday morning by sticking his nose in my ear and sniffing loudly. I grinned before remembering that Mr. Babin was coming home from the hospital today. I stopped smiling. I rolled over and buried my face in Gus's fur. He let me love on him for a minute, but he got impatient quick and left my side to scratch on my door.

Gus devoured the scrambled eggs I made him for breakfast, but I only picked at mine. Nana Pat didn't even remind me that it was the most important meal of the day. She didn't say much at all, as a matter of fact. Papaw Jack wasn't eating much either.

Afterward, I sat on the back porch and watched Gus sniff his way around the yard. Once he was certain the perimeter was secure, he sat in his favorite spot. He watched the birds. He tilted his head back and smelled the wind. I wondered what he was thinking about. Could he feel the goodbye coming?

I sat in a shady spot on the grass. Gus came to lay next to me. I tried to memorize everything about him. The way his tail curved over his back when he was alert. The way his ears swayed, how he sometimes kicked them when he was trailing, how they floated in his water bowl.

The way he was always happy to see me.

"You're my very best friend. You know that, right?"

He looked up at me with his mournful eyes. His face was the mushiest when he was lying down that way. I lay down next to him, my head next to his. I didn't mind his hound smell. It smelled like home.

"You're going to have to go back to your house now," I told him. "I wish I could keep you, but you aren't mine." But that wasn't true. He was my heart. "Mr. Babin misses you. And I'm sure you miss him and your own yard." Was I a horrible person if I wished Gus would miss me the most?

My chest felt hollow, like someone had punched a hole right through the middle of it. I couldn't imagine not waking up to Gus snuffling my ear. I would miss his singing so very much. I had never had someone want to be with me as much as Gus wanted to be with me. It had been nice, being wanted. Being loved.

He made me feel like I deserved those things.

Gus sat up and licked the tears off my face. "Thanks, buddy," I said. "You always know how to make me feel better."

Life seemed very unfair just then. It just kept taking things away.

"I'm going to ask Mr. Babin to let me take you on walks." I couldn't stand the idea that Gus would think I left him. "Thanks for finding me, Gus." He would never understand how much I'd needed him this summer. "I'm going to miss you so much."

Papaw Jack came outside a little while later and sat on the bench. We didn't talk, but it was nice not having to go through this alone.

Gus, who had been peering through the fence into Mrs. Gill's yard, sat down in front of Papaw Jack. He rubbed Gus's ears. "Good boy," he said. "The very best." Papaw Jack pulled a treat out of his pocket and gave it to Gus.

"Are you going with us?" I asked.

"Goodbyes are hard."

They were the worst.

"But I'll be there." His words had weight.

And then it was time to go.

We drove even though it wasn't that far of a walk. I sat in the back of the truck with Gus. He stuck his head out the window and let his ears flap in the breeze.

My heart sank as we pulled up in front of Mr. Babin's house and I saw a FOR SALE sign. It looked like this was a forever goodbye after all.

"You are the very best boy," I told Gus for the thousandth time. "I love you so much."

I didn't want to get out of the truck. I didn't want to let him go. But I didn't have a choice.

I wiped my face. I didn't want Mr. Babin seeing how upset I was.

Nana Pat and Papaw Jack walked to the front door with us. Nana Pat knocked. Papaw Jack rested a veined and gnarled hand on top of Gus's head.

It wasn't Mr. Babin who answered the door. "Gus!" The man squatted down and rubbed Gus's ears. Gus's tail went wild and then he was pushing his way past the man and into the house, leaving me standing on the front porch. "And you must be Glory. I'm David, Homer's son. Come on in."

"We're going to wait here," Nana Pat said.

David glanced at me before nodding at Nana Pat. "I'll join you." He turned to me. "Dad's in the living room."

Mr. Babin was sitting in his recliner, smiling and laughing as Gus rested his paws on the seat of the chair and tried to climb into his lap.

"You're too big for that," Mr. Babin was telling Gus. He saw me then. "Glory!" Gus dropped to the floor but didn't leave Mr. Babin's side. "Where are your grandparents?"

"Outside with your son."

Mr. Babin rubbed Gus's ears and underneath his chin in Gus's ticklish spot. Gus's back leg twitched, and Mr. Babin and I smiled at each other.

"Has he been good?"

"The best." I was trying so very hard not to cry again. "He found a lost little boy. Did you hear?"

Mr. Babin's eyes widened. "I had not heard."

I told him all about teaching Gus to track and his finding Sebastian. I told him about finding Judy's kittens and how much Gus loved mornings. I kept talking, knowing that once I stopped, I would have to say goodbye. But finally, I ran out of words.

Mr. Babin smiled at me, then looked down at Gus, his face so very full of love. "Sounds like you've had a good summer."

The best, I thought. When it should have been the worst.

Gus did that. Gus had been there for me when I'd needed a friend. "He missed you. He was sad a lot."

"Bloodhounds look sad all the time."

"I was going to ask if you needed me to take Gus on walks, but . . ." I cleared my throat. "You're moving?"

Mr. Babin's mouth twisted, his wrinkles rising and falling until his face looked like the Mississippi River on a windy day, wavy and mad. "I'm going into assisted living." His mouth formed the words as if they had nettles and thorns on them. Then his face relaxed, and he gave me a small smile. "It's time." He lowered his voice to a whisper. "I didn't tell my son this, but I set the kitchen on fire in January. Just a little one," he added, probably because I looked so worried. "My wife was the cook anyway."

He reached out and put his hand on Gus's head. Gus shifted closer to the chair. "You're the best boy, but they won't let me have a dog at my new place. And Gus wouldn't want to be cooped up there anyway." Mr. Babin rubbed Gus's ear and Gus grunted and leaned into his hand. "I have a very important question to ask you, Glory."

My heart did a little tango of hope.

"Do you think you might want to keep Gus? Forever?"

I was furious when my eyes filled with tears, then less so when Mr. Babin's did too.

The *yes* was already sitting on my tongue, just waiting to jump right out of my mouth. I pressed my lips tight together to prevent it from escaping. "But you'll be lonely," I finally said.

"I will miss him very much. But I don't think I'll be lonely. Lots of other people live there."

"Won't he miss you?"

Mr. Babin smiled. "Maybe for a time. But he has you, and I can tell how much he loves you. Even if I could take him back, he would miss you too. Sometimes we do things that will make us sad if they are the best for those we love." He let us sit with that sentence for a moment. "And Gus living with you is the best thing for him. I can't take care of him anymore. Not like he deserves." He rested his hand on Gus's head. "Would you like to have Gus?"

"Yes, please." Gus and I belonged together. He was going to be sad without Mr. Babin. I could help him through that. We understood each other. My heart sang *Mine, mine, mine.*

"You'll need to ask your grandparents. It's a big thing I'm asking."

But I already knew they'd say yes. I saw how unhappy they were this morning. We all loved Gus.

"I'll go talk to them right now," I said. I also wanted to give him some time alone with Gus.

I heard Mr. Babin murmuring to Gus as I slipped out the door.

"He wants me to keep Gus!" I blurted out as soon as I was outside. My ribs felt both bigger and smaller. "Forever."

Nana Pat and Papaw Jack were both smiling. "David told us," Nana Pat said.

"So it's okay? I can adopt him?" I crossed both fingers and rested them in the small of my back.

"I don't figure I could stop you even if I wanted to." Nana Pat grimaced slightly. "Though your dad might be mad I said yes without talking to him."

Papaw Jack winked. "Wouldn't be the first time she's made someone mad."

But I knew Dad wouldn't be mad. Gus made everyone's hearts bigger somehow.

I went back inside. Mr. Babin wasn't talking to Gus anymore, just silently stroking his head. Gus's eyes were closed. They both looked like they wanted to fall asleep.

"They said yes."

Mr. Babin looked relieved. "Good. You know I'm not abandoning him."

"I know that."

"I wouldn't trust him with just anyone."

He'd picked me to take care of someone he loved. I'd never felt so special in all my life.

"He'll have a good life with you."

"The best," I promised. "He's already my best friend."

"I love you, boy," he told Gus. "Go have adventures."

Mr. Babin looked tired then, and I knew it was time to go. "If you like, I can call you sometimes, at your new place, or send a letter. Maybe we could even come by for a visit, like we did at the hospital. Only you could come outside. That way you'll know how Gus is doing."

"I would love for y'all to come see me," he said. "But I'm not worried. I know he'll be just fine."

"Then when we visit, he'll get to see that you're doing just fine too."

Mr. Babin smiled. "I'd like that."

I led Gus to the front door. "Thank you, Mr. Babin."

"Thank you, Glory. Bye, boy." Mr. Babin turned his face toward the window, maybe so he wouldn't have to see Gus leave.

Mr. Babin loved Gus so much that he would do anything to give him his very best life, even if that life wasn't with him.

I hadn't understood how letting something go could be a form of love, but I did now.

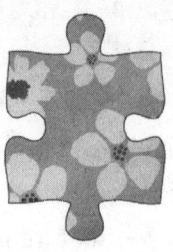

CHAPTER TWENTY

It was still dark when my alarm went off. Groggy, I reached over and turned it off, but then I remembered why I was getting up so early on a Sunday, and I sat up in bed, suddenly wide awake.

Today was our first tracking trial.

I threw off the covers and turned on the lamp next to my bed. Gus grunted and stretched but didn't wake up. His new bed had a pillow that ran along three sides, but mostly he slept with his head on the floor, ears flopped over his eyes like his very own sleep mask.

"Good morning, Gus." His tail thumped against his bed even though he didn't open his eyes. "It's my turn to wake you up." I rubbed his belly. He snorted. "Want some breakfast?"

That did the trick. He rolled to his feet and whined a little when I took too long pulling on a sweatshirt. I was getting fluent in Gus.

Dad was pouring himself coffee when we came in the kitchen. "Big day," he said.

"Don't make him nervous."

Dad smiled over the rim of his mug. "Gus has more confidence than anyone I've ever met."

He was right. "Fine. Don't make me nervous."

Gus bounded down the steps and into the backyard. The air was still warm, but there was a feel of October in it. The first thing Dad had done after buying Mr. Babin's house was repair the steps. Then he'd made the gate Gus-proof.

And now Gus and I were both at home.

Nana Pat and Papaw Jack showed up thirty minutes later. Papaw Jack was carrying a box wrapped in plaid paper and tied with a big red bow. "Hey, buddy," he said as Gus ran over to tell him hello.

Gus sure had a lot of people loving him. Every morning after I left for school, Papaw Jack walked down and picked up Gus. Then they walked back to his house and spent the day together so that neither of them was lonely. I'd been worried at first that Gus might pull Papaw Jack down, but as impatient and stubborn as Gus was, he was gentle with Papaw Jack.

"I bought y'all something." Papaw Jack handed me the box. Up close, the wrapping paper was lumpy and the bow was a little crooked. "I wrapped it myself."

I let Gus sniff it before I tore it open. Nana Pat was smiling. Dad looked curious. Gus, helpful as always, snatched the bow, but he spit it out immediately when he realized it wasn't edible.

I opened the lid. Inside, nestled in white tissue paper, was a leather harness. I took it out of the box. *Gus* was stamped into the leather on the side.

"It's beautiful," I breathed. It was the nicest present anyone had ever given Gus.

"You don't have to use it today," Papaw Jack said. "He might need to get used to it first. But I wanted to give it to you today." He patted the top of Gus's head. "He's come a long way."

Nana Pat smiled at Dad. "I think we all have."

"Thank you." Gus would absolutely be wearing this today.

The drive to Mead didn't take very long. Gus hung his head out the window to catch every single scent between Sweet Olive and there, but I sat with my knees to my chest, my insides twisted into impossible knots. Papaw Jack and Nana Pat followed in their own car after picking up Aunt Kat and Mervin, who were coming for moral support.

The field that had been turned into a parking lot was almost full when we got there. I buckled on Gus's new harness. It fit perfectly. "You look so handsome." Gus tossed his head, as if to make it clear that he was always handsome.

"It fits!" Papaw Jack said as we met in the parking lot.

Mervin was ecstatic to see Gus, and they bounced around each other before I tugged Gus away.

We had a tracking trial to pass.

"Starting to feel like October," a man behind me in line said. The air was a bit drier. I nodded politely, too nervous to do anything else but wait my turn to pick up our entry packets.

Gus, on the other hand, didn't seem nervous at all. He sniffed dogs and people alike, his tail wagging happily as he made new friends.

My palms were sweaty as I stepped up to the registration table. "Glory St. Romain," I said. "And Gus."

The woman looked down at her list, riffled through some packets, and handed me a large envelope with my name on it. "Good luck," she said, smiling up at me and then down at Gus.

Handlers, dogs, and the audience stood together in the dewy grass. Most of the other handlers were older than my dad even, but there were a couple of teenagers in the line. We smiled at each other nervously.

And then I caught sight of a familiar face. "Ms. Caroline!" I said, rushing over. She was wearing her purple-and-gold sweater, and Gus managed to get a little drool on it again. "You came!"

"Of course," she said, smiling at me and obediently rubbing Gus's ears. "I wouldn't miss you and Gus in action for the world."

Gus gave a loud bark, and suddenly we were surrounded by Hymels. Lydie threw her arms around Gus's neck, and Sebastian patted Gus's chest.

"I was afraid we weren't going to make it," Rosemary said. "We got lost on the way here."

"We did not get lost," her dad said. As usual, his hair was sticking up. But he had managed to get his shirt buttoned straight. "I took the scenic route."

Mrs. Hymel laughed. "I've seen every scenic route in every state we've been to."

"He went the wrong way down a one-way," Rosemary whispered.

My insides felt all warm and fluttery. Used to, I'd be the only kid without family at school events. Now I had a slew of people who'd shown up for me.

A woman in jeans and a T-shirt with a dog on it strode forward. I turned around and got still. The woman didn't have a mic, but we could hear her just fine. "Unlike in other competitions where the handler is in charge, in tracking, the dog is in charge."

"Who is she telling?" I muttered to Gus. "You are even bossier than Nana Pat."

"I heard that," Nana Pat grumbled.

"This is a pass-or-fail competition, so no points for style," the woman said, and the crowd chuckled.

"We'd have them beat in style, I believe," Papaw Jack whispered.

We drew numbers. Gus and I were right in the middle. There was no time limit, so each dog took its own time. We all clapped when a dog passed. The first time the whistle was blown for a dog, which meant he'd lost the trail and had failed, we all groaned a little under our breath.

"Just have fun," Dad told me. "That's the whole point."

And he was right. Spending time with Gus was the best part about the whole thing. But I wanted us to pass.

Mom wasn't there, of course. I still hadn't heard anything from her since the postcard. I'd mostly stopped looking for her face in a crowd. But rather than being sad about who wasn't there, I instead felt joy at who was. My mom was gone. But many more people had stepped up, and I had an even bigger family than I could have ever imagined.

And then it was our turn. I put on my tracking gloves, which helped me get a better grip on the lead, and walked Gus to the start. "Find it," I told him.

He took off. The judges were roaming the area but staying well away from the trail. There were no flags, so I had to trust Gus completely. That wasn't so hard. Gus churned ahead, nose to the ground, and I thought about all the other things Gus had found this summer.

Me. He'd been my very first friend in Sweet Olive. And even though I'd been in charge and taking care of him, I thought I'd needed him more than he'd needed me.

Mrs. Gill's kittens. They all had good homes, including the ginger cat named Leo that slept in Rosemary's bed. Her parents had softened on pets since Gus found Sebastian.

Gus had helped Papaw Jack find himself again, had led him back to his garden and shop.

And then we were there. A battered leather wallet sat on the ground, and Gus gave the sign. My little cheering section erupted. "Good boy, Gus!" I said, grinning, falling to my knees and rubbing his ears. "What a good boy! Mr. Babin will be so proud!"

I'd written him a couple of letters once he'd gotten settled into his new place. He'd sent me and Gus a good luck card. We were going for our first visit next week.

"I knew you could do it," I told Gus. It hadn't mattered that he was fully grown before he'd started training, that he'd been lost too, in a way, and found by a new family when his old one fell apart.

And what had I found this summer? I had found my family, the one I already had but didn't really know, and friends who were just as good as family.

I glanced at my crowd of people.

I'd found where I belonged.

ACKNOWLEDGMENTS

I am lucky to have so many supportive people in my life. I want to thank my phenomenal agent, Alice Sutherland-Hawes of ASH Literary, for all her hard work and cheerleading. Thank you to my incredible editors, Kate Meltzer and Emilia Sowersby, for their enthusiasm and excitement for this story. Thanks also to the team at MacKids and Roaring Brook Press—L. Whitt, Kristen Stedman, Jennifer Healey, Alexa Blanco, Connie Hsu, Allison Verost, and countless more. I am forever grateful to the talented Madi Wong for this adorable cover.

Thanks to Abigail Johnson and Kate Goodwin for letting me bounce ideas off them and panic (and celebrate) in their inboxes. I am especially grateful for all the time they have spent giving me honest and insightful feedback. They believed on the days I didn't.

I want to thank all the teachers and librarians out there who put books in the hands of students. I want to especially thank a former teacher of mine, Rosemary Harris, who passed away before she could hold this book in her hands. I am disappointed she will never know I named a character after her. Mrs. Harris was my high-school gifted teacher, as well as my drama teacher, oratory coach, Beta sponsor, mentor, and friend. Since her passing, I have found numerous letters she wrote me over my high school years, and I have been moved all over again at what a special person she truly was. Smart, tough, and classy, she was everything I wanted to be, and while I am not even half the teacher she was, I hope I have taken some of her spirit into the classroom with me. I know I am better for having known her.

This story would not exist without the love of a dog. My first bloodhound, Gus, was a red bloodhound just like this fictional Gus. He was the best boy I could have ever asked for. He was funny and mischievous and I still miss him every day. I am thankful to my current dogs, Ellie and Oscar, for their company while I wrangle words. It's easier writing about good dogs when you are surrounded by them.

Thank you to my family for their unwavering support. Thanks to my parents and my grandmother for brainstorming titles with me. Sorry, Dad, that yours wasn't chosen. Thanks to my sister for all her hilarious texts, for letting me pick her librarian brain, and for absolutely always being there.

And to my husband, who convinced me we needed enormous slobbering dogs in the house. You were right. They do make everything better. As do you.